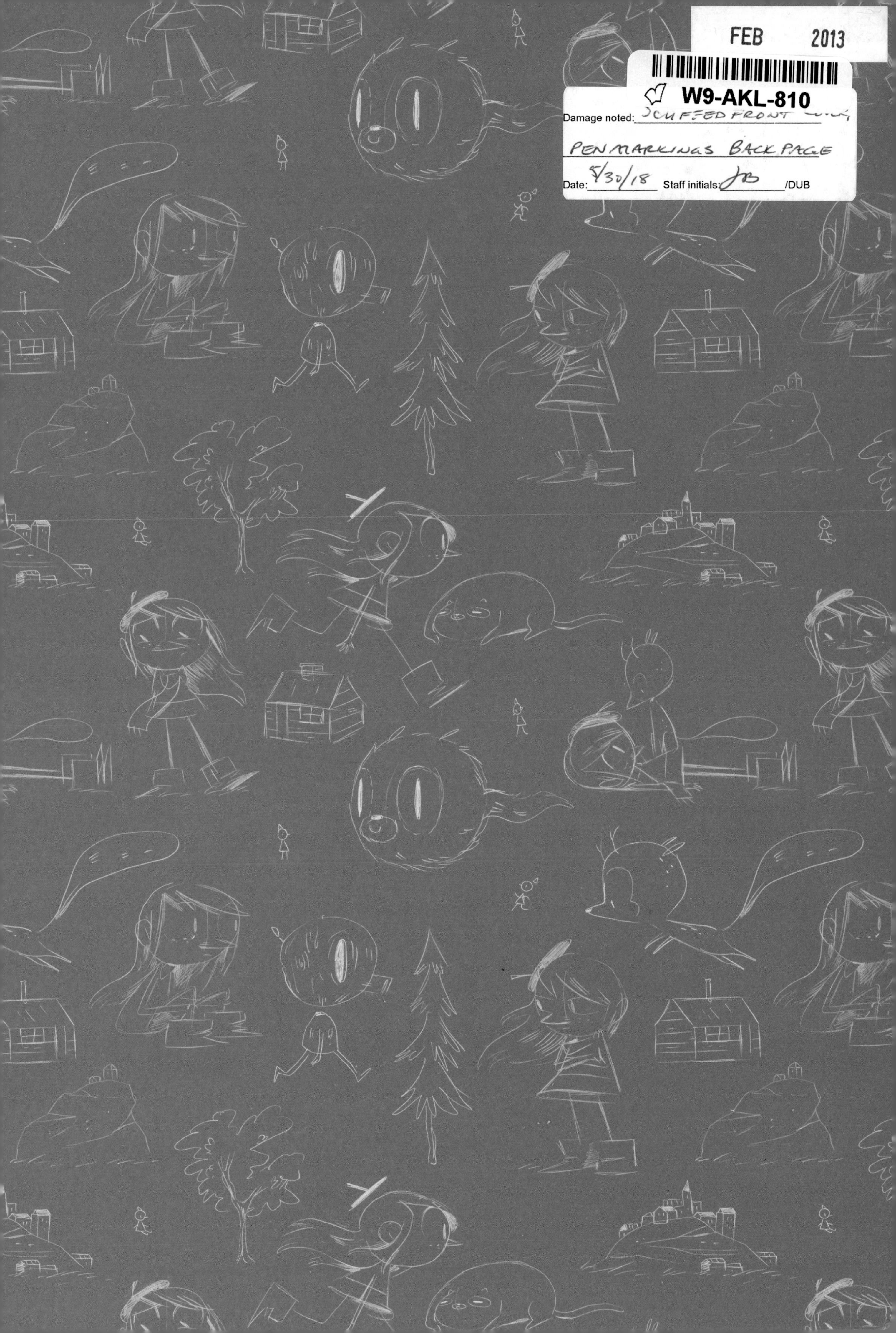

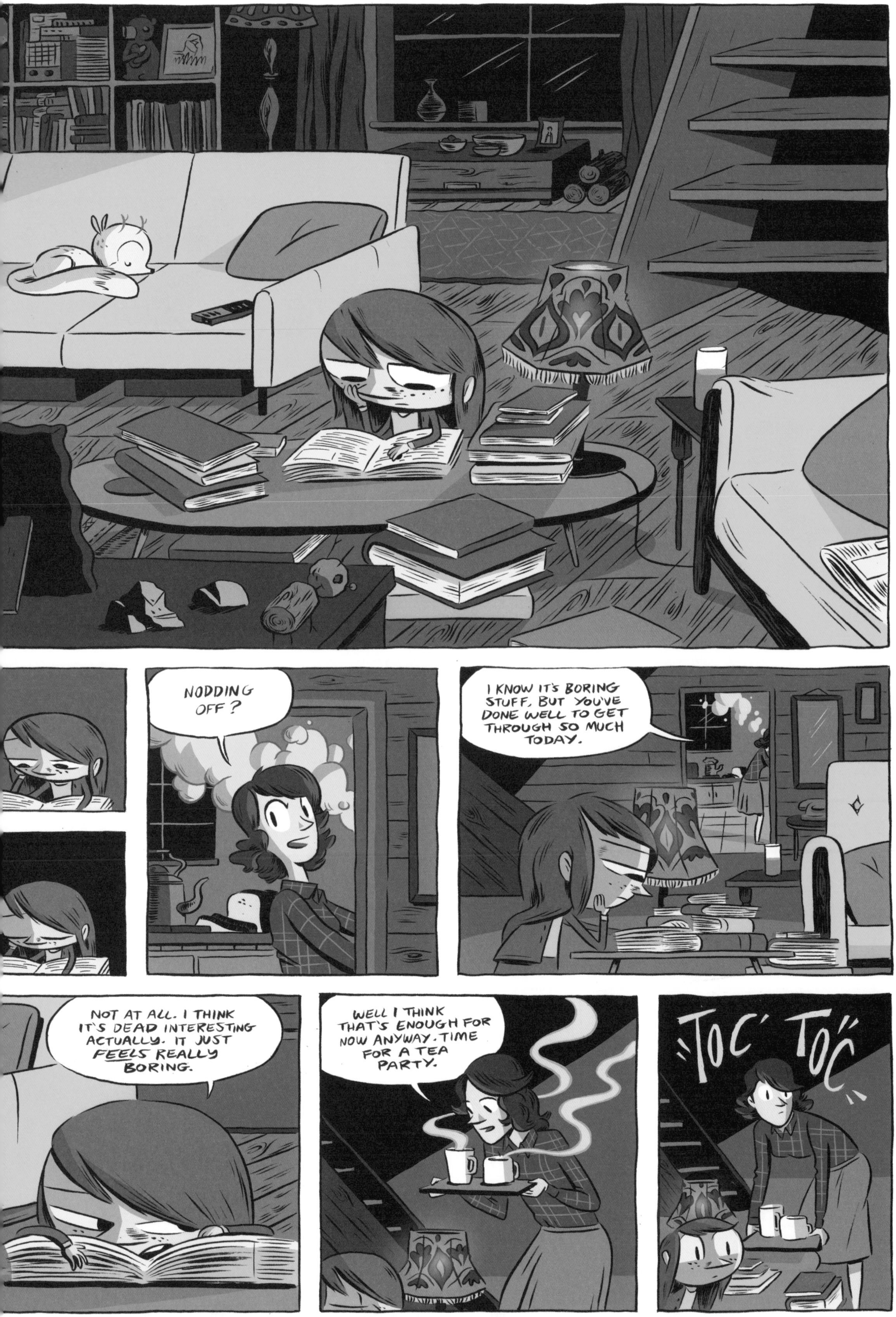
NODDING OFF?
I KNOW IT'S BORING STUFF, BUT YOU'VE DONE WELL TO GET THROUGH SO MUCH TODAY.
NOT AT ALL. I THINK IT'S DEAD INTERESTING ACTUALLY. IT JUST FEELS REALLY BORING.
WELL I THINK THAT'S ENOUGH FOR NOW ANYWAY. TIME FOR A TEA PARTY.
TOC TOC

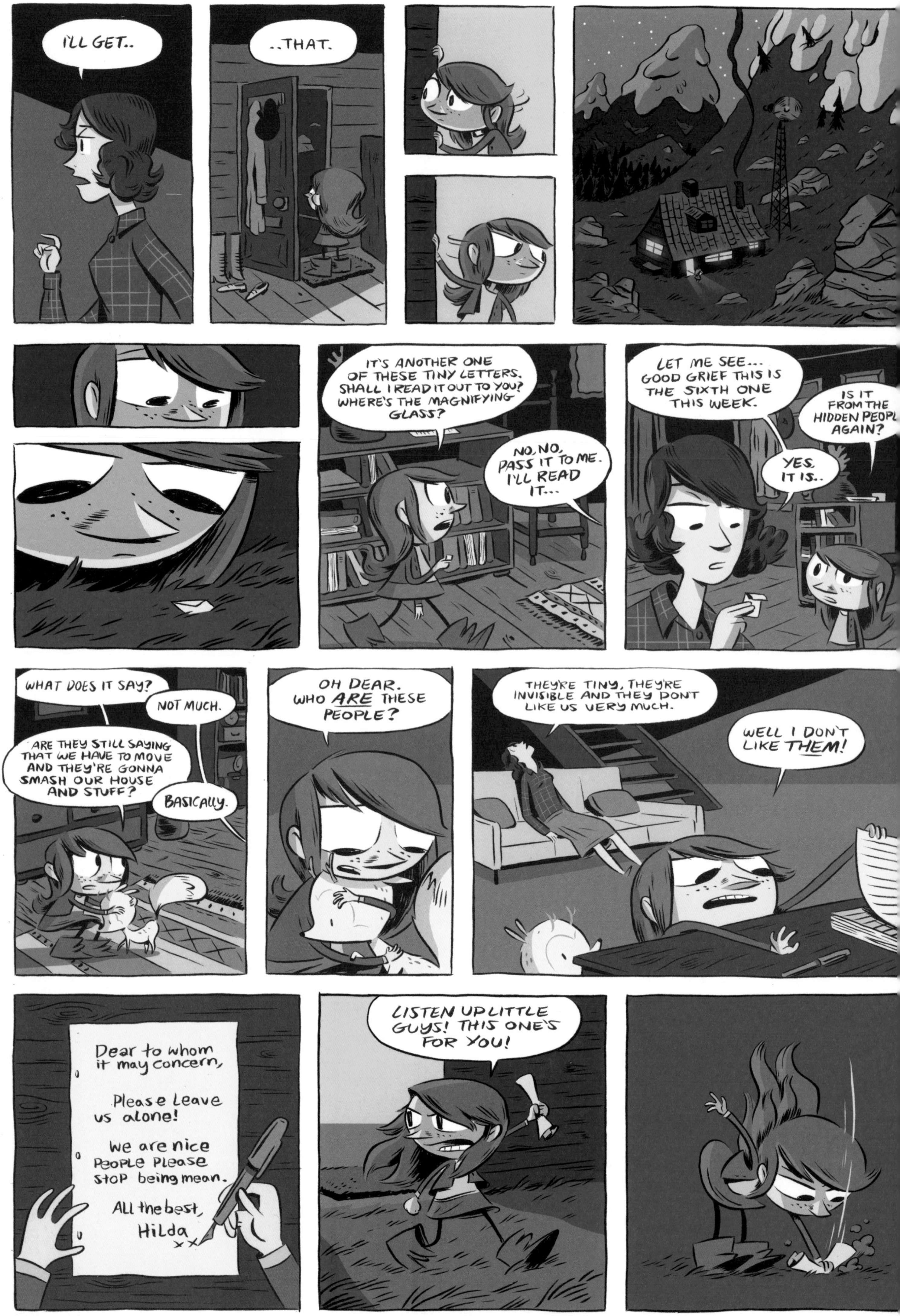
I'LL GET..
..THAT.
IT'S ANOTHER ONE OF THESE TINY LETTERS. SHALL I READ IT OUT TO YOU? WHERE'S THE MAGNIFYING GLASS?
NO, NO, PASS IT TO ME. I'LL READ IT...
LET ME SEE... GOOD GRIEF THIS IS THE SIXTH ONE THIS WEEK.
IS IT FROM THE HIDDEN PEOPL AGAIN?
YES. IT IS..
WHAT DOES IT SAY?
NOT MUCH.
ARE THEY STILL SAYING THAT WE HAVE TO MOVE AND THEY'RE GONNA SMASH OUR HOUSE AND STUFF?
BASICALLY.
OH DEAR. WHO ARE THESE PEOPLE?
THEY'RE TINY, THEY'RE INVISIBLE AND THEY DON'T LIKE US VERY MUCH.
WELL I DON'T LIKE THEM!
Dear to whom it may concern,
Please leave us alone!
We are nice people please stop being mean.
All the best,
Hilda xx
LISTEN UP LITTLE GUYS! THIS ONE'S FOR YOU!

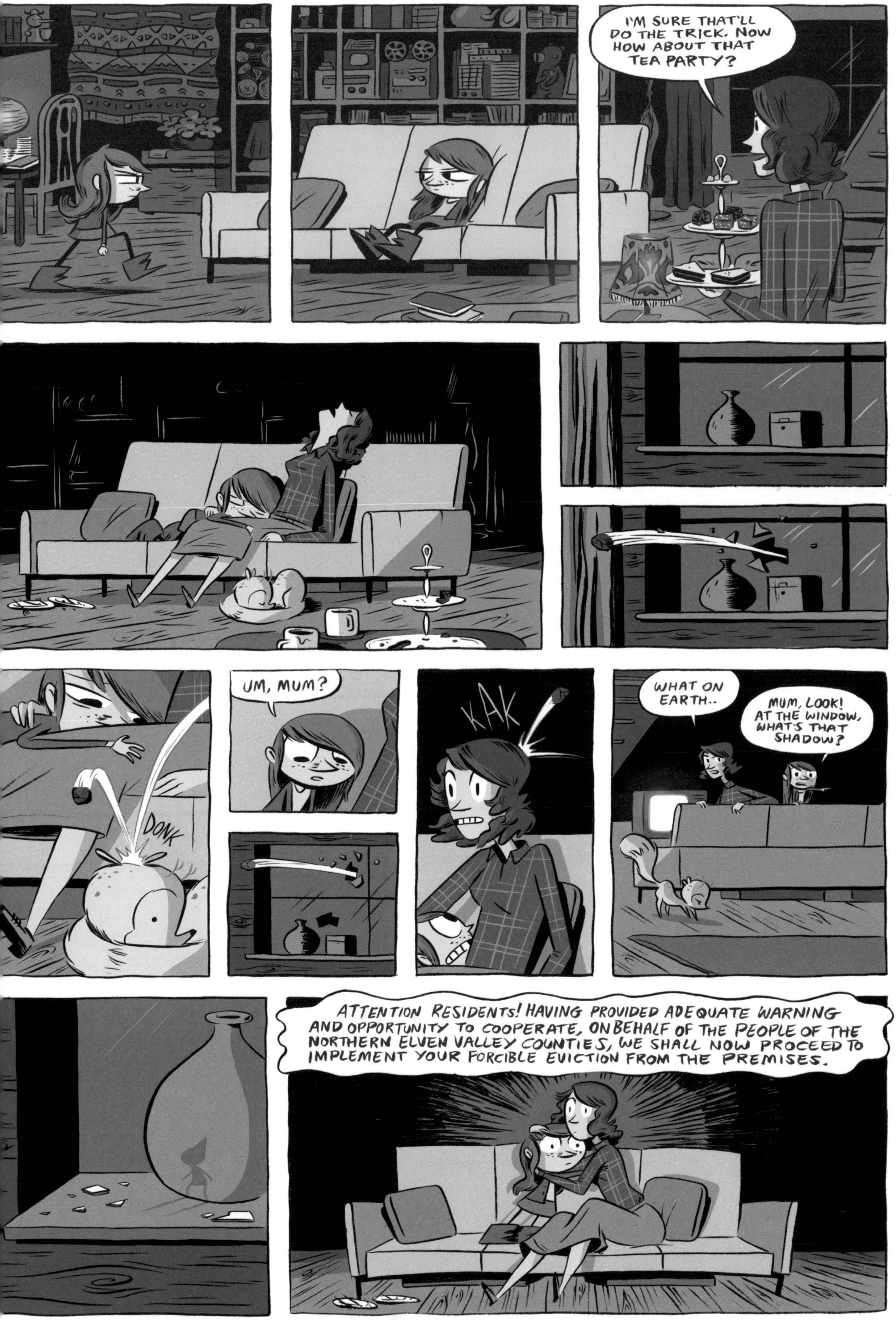
I'M SURE THAT'LL DO THE TRICK. NOW HOW ABOUT THAT TEA PARTY?
UM, MUM?
KAK
DONK
WHAT ON EARTH..
MUM, LOOK! AT THE WINDOW, WHAT'S THAT SHADOW?
ATTENTION RESIDENTS! HAVING PROVIDED ADEQUATE WARNING AND OPPORTUNITY TO COOPERATE, ON BEHALF OF THE PEOPLE OF THE NORTHERN ELVEN VALLEY COUNTIES, WE SHALL NOW PROCEED TO IMPLEMENT YOUR FORCIBLE EVICTION FROM THE PREMISES.

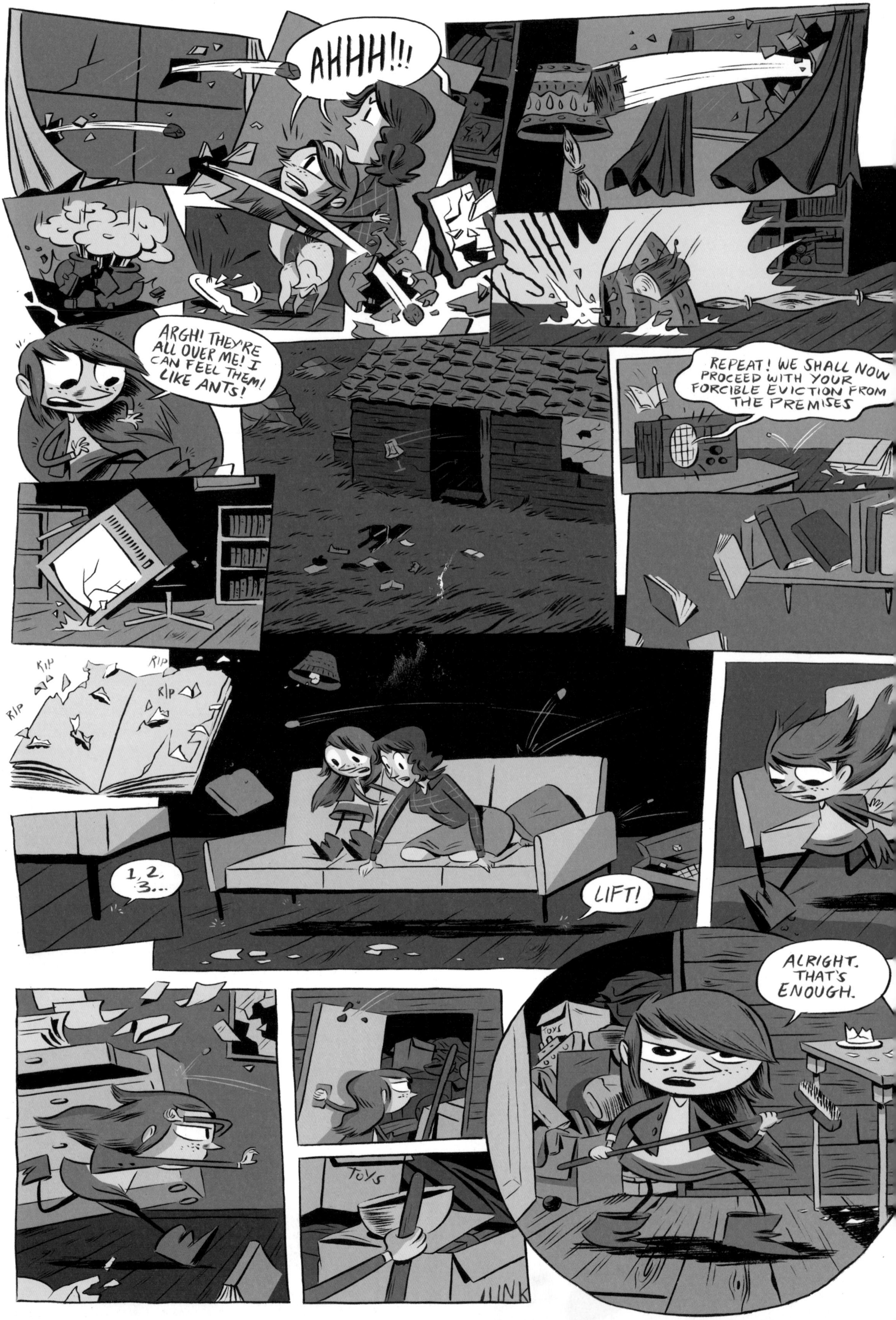
AHHH!!!
THH
ARGH! THEY'RE ALL OVER ME! I CAN FEEL THEM! LIKE ANTS!
REPEAT! WE SHALL NOW PROCEED WITH YOUR FORCIBLE EVICTION FROM THE PREMISES
RIP
RIP
RIP
RIP
1, 2, 3...
LIFT!
ALRIGHT. THAT'S ENOUGH.
TOYS
TOYS
LINK

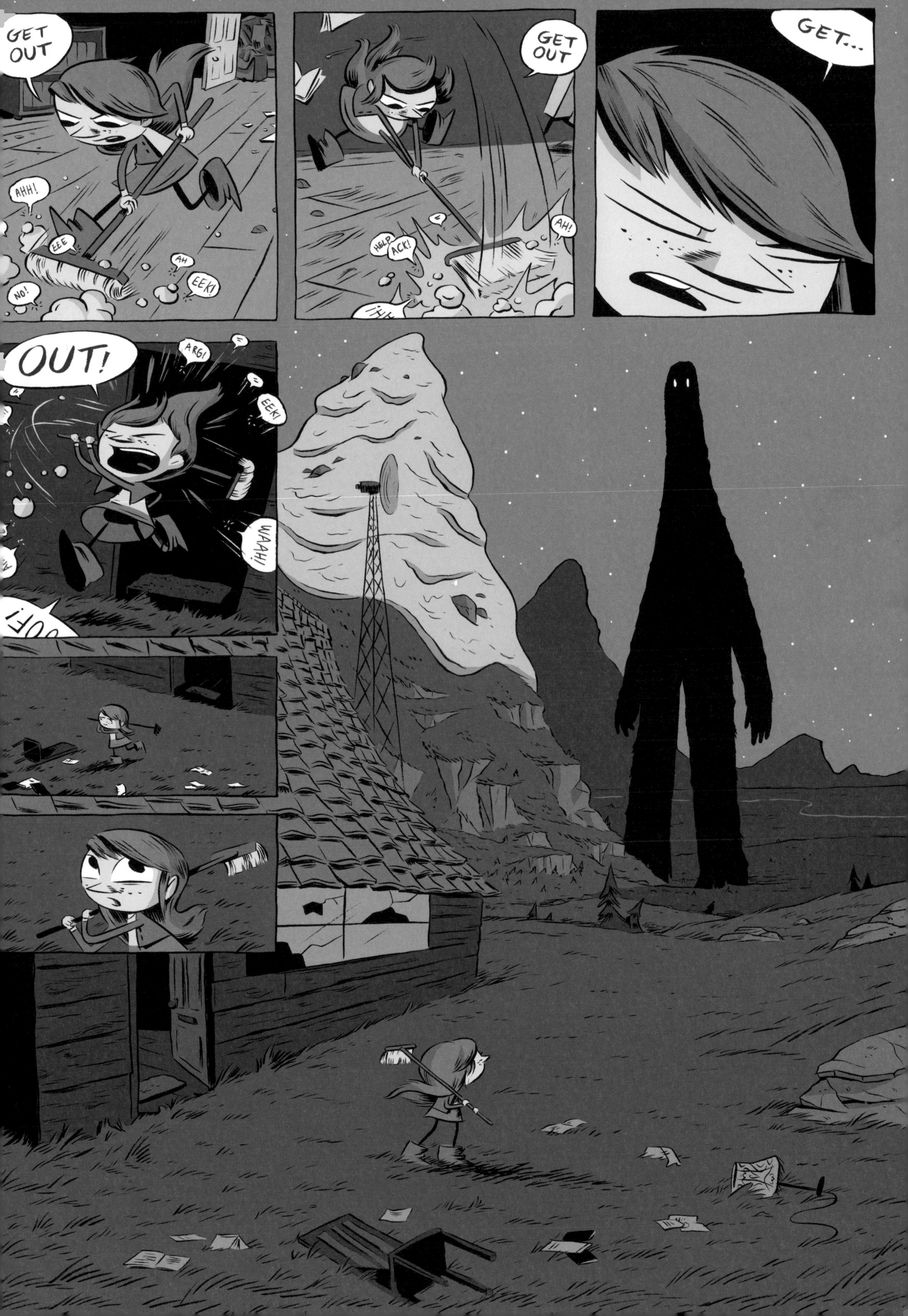
GET OUT
AHH!
EEE
AH
EEK!
NO!
GET OUT
HELP
ACK!
AH!
GET...
OUT!
ARG!
EEK!
WAAH!

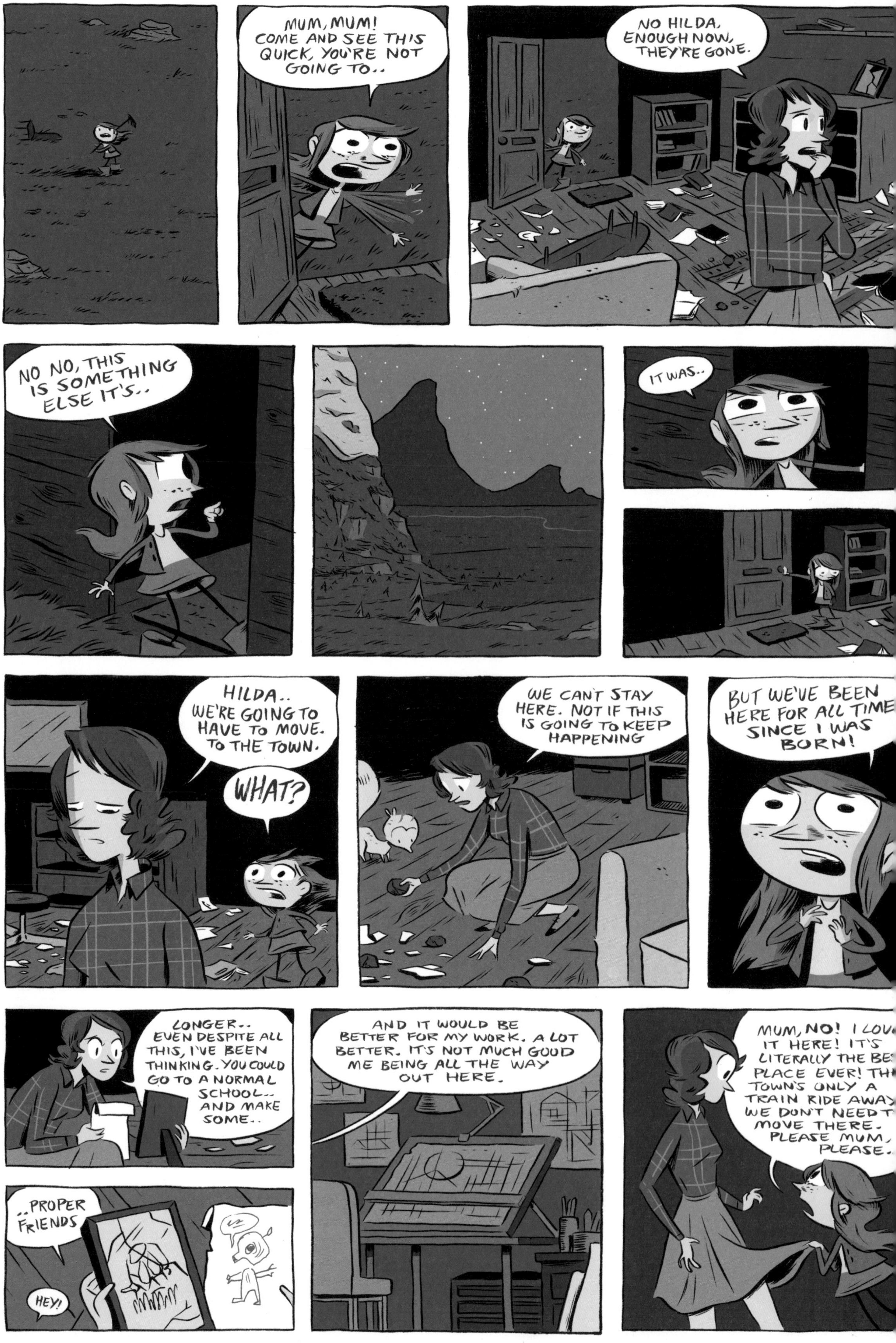
MUM, MUM! COME AND SEE THIS QUICK, YOU'RE NOT GOING TO..
NO HILDA, ENOUGH NOW, THEY'RE GONE.
NO NO, THIS IS SOMETHING ELSE IT'S..
IT WAS..
HILDA.. WE'RE GOING TO HAVE TO MOVE. TO THE TOWN.
WHAT?
WE CAN'T STAY HERE. NOT IF THIS IS GOING TO KEEP HAPPENING
BUT WE'VE BEEN HERE FOR ALL TIME SINCE I WAS BORN!
LONGER.. EVEN DESPITE ALL THIS, I'VE BEEN THINKING. YOU COULD GO TO A NORMAL SCHOOL.. AND MAKE SOME..
..PROPER FRIENDS
HEY!
AND IT WOULD BE BETTER FOR MY WORK. A LOT BETTER. IT'S NOT MUCH GOOD ME BEING ALL THE WAY OUT HERE.
MUM, NO! I LOV IT HERE! IT'S LITERALLY THE BE PLACE EVER! TH TOWN'S ONLY A TRAIN RIDE AWAY WE DON'T NEED T MOVE THERE. PLEASE MUM, PLEASE.

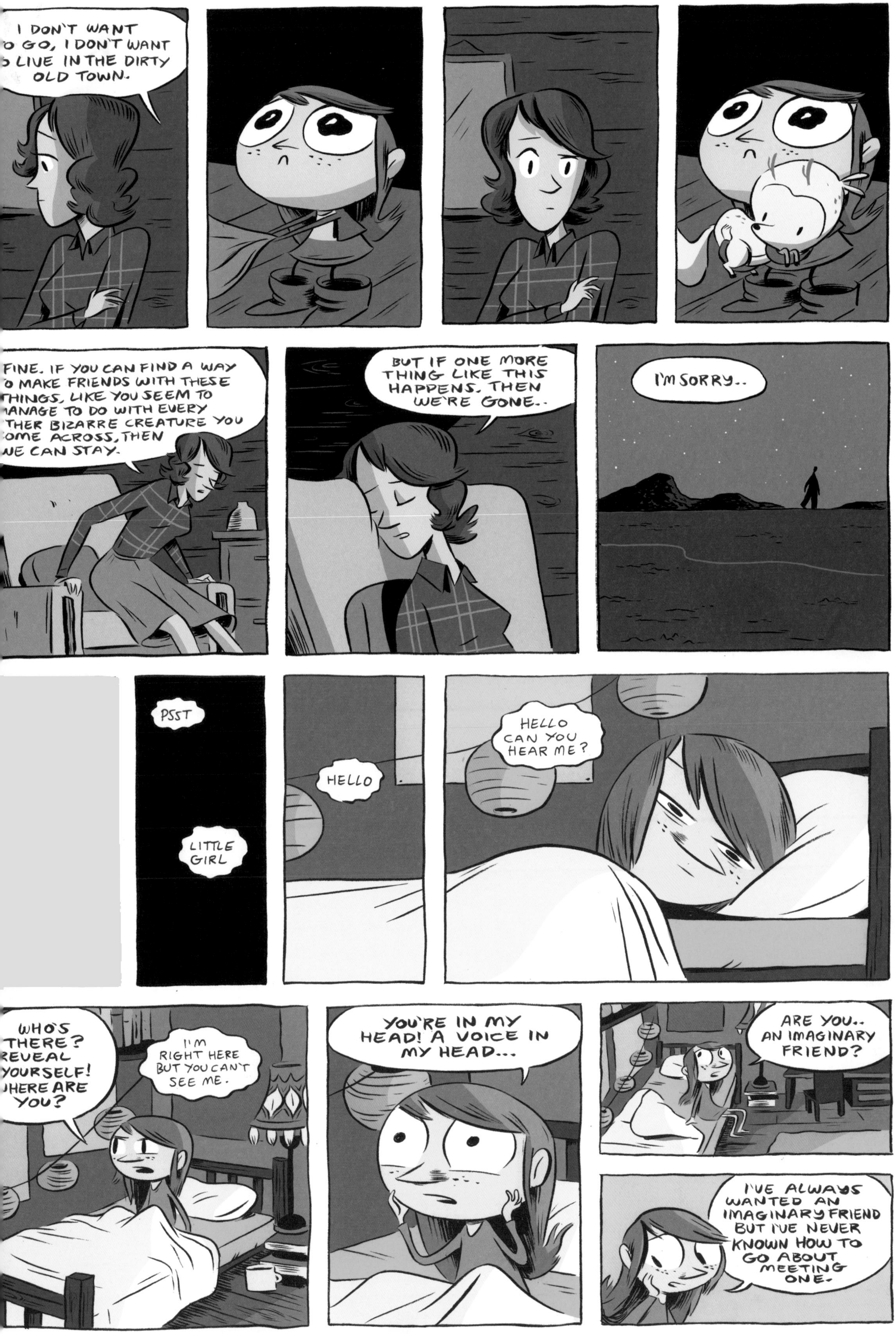
I DON'T WANT
O GO, I DON'T WANT
O LIVE IN THE DIRTY
OLD TOWN.
FINE. IF YOU CAN FIND A WAY
O MAKE FRIENDS WITH THESE
THINGS, LIKE YOU SEEM TO
ANAGE TO DO WITH EVERY
THER BIZARRE CREATURE YOU
OME ACROSS, THEN
E CAN STAY.
BUT IF ONE MORE THING LIKE THIS HAPPENS, THEN WE'RE GONE..
I'M SORRY..
PSST
LITTLE GIRL
HELLO
HELLO CAN YOU HEAR ME?
WHO'S
THERE?
REVEAL
YOURSELF!
HERE ARE
YOU?
I'M RIGHT HERE BUT YOU CAN'T SEE ME.
YOU'RE IN MY HEAD! A VOICE IN MY HEAD...
ARE YOU.. AN IMAGINARY FRIEND?
I'VE ALWAYS WANTED AN IMAGINARY FRIEND BUT I'VE NEVER KNOWN HOW TO GO ABOUT MEETING ONE.

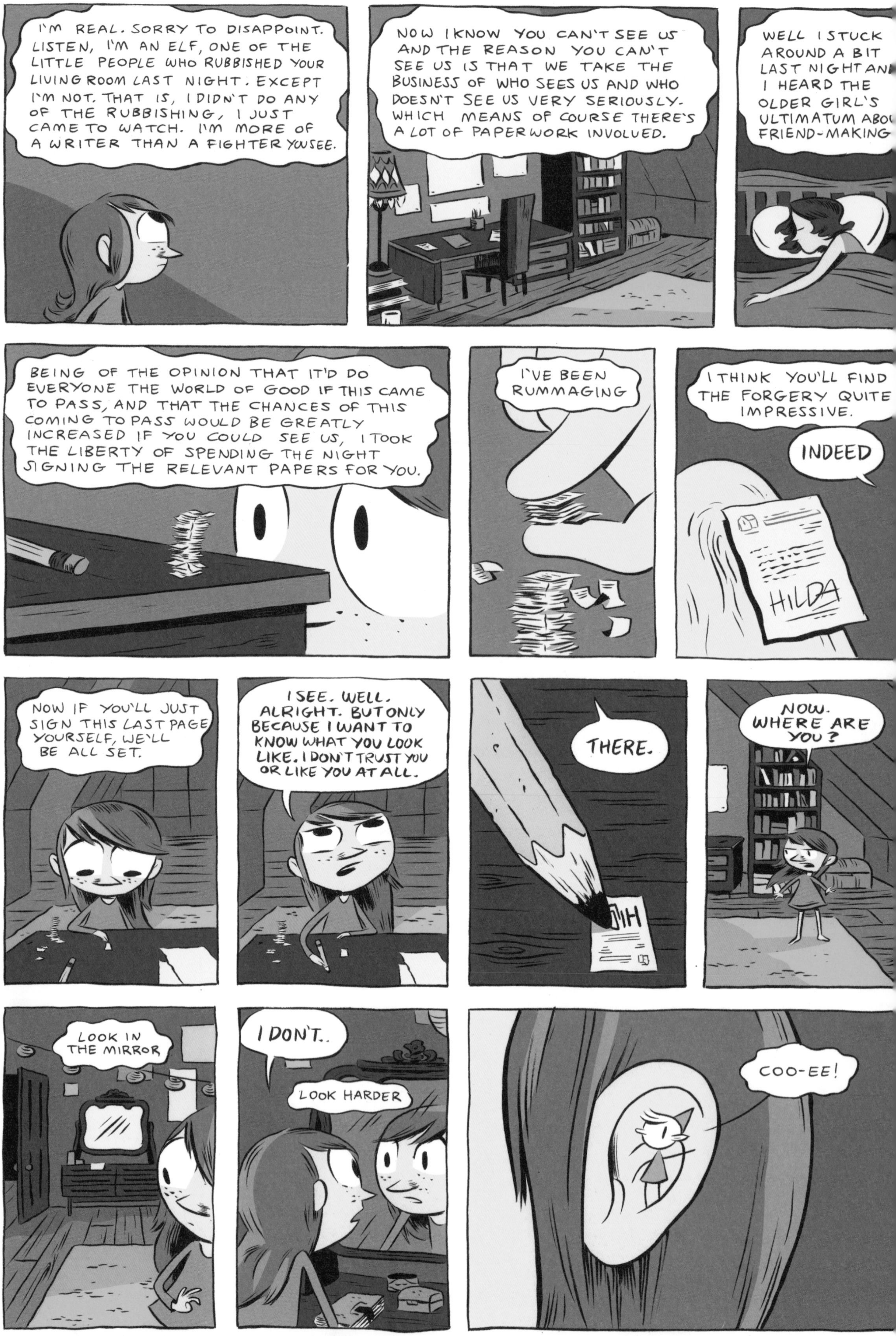
I'M REAL. SORRY TO DISAPPOINT. LISTEN, I'M AN ELF, ONE OF THE LITTLE PEOPLE WHO RUBBISHED YOUR LIVING ROOM LAST NIGHT. EXCEPT I'M NOT. THAT IS, I DIDN'T DO ANY OF THE RUBBISHING, I JUST CAME TO WATCH. I'M MORE OF A WRITER THAN A FIGHTER YOU SEE.
NOW I KNOW YOU CAN'T SEE US AND THE REASON YOU CAN'T SEE US IS THAT WE TAKE THE BUSINESS OF WHO SEES US AND WHO DOESN'T SEE US VERY SERIOUSLY. WHICH MEANS OF COURSE THERE'S A LOT OF PAPERWORK INVOLVED.
WELL I STUCK AROUND A BIT LAST NIGHT AN I HEARD THE OLDER GIRL'S ULTIMATUM ABO FRIEND-MAKING
BEING OF THE OPINION THAT IT'D DO EVERYONE THE WORLD OF GOOD IF THIS CAME TO PASS, AND THAT THE CHANCES OF THIS COMING TO PASS WOULD BE GREATLY INCREASED IF YOU COULD SEE US, I TOOK THE LIBERTY OF SPENDING THE NIGHT SIGNING THE RELEVANT PAPERS FOR YOU.
I'VE BEEN RUMMAGING
I THINK YOU'LL FIND THE FORGERY QUITE IMPRESSIVE.
INDEED
HILDA
NOW IF YOU'LL JUST SIGN THIS LAST PAGE YOURSELF, WE'LL BE ALL SET.
I SEE. WELL. ALRIGHT. BUT ONLY BECAUSE I WANT TO KNOW WHAT YOU LOOK LIKE. I DON'T TRUST YOU OR LIKE YOU AT ALL.
THERE.
NOW. WHERE ARE YOU?
LOOK IN THE MIRROR
I DON'T..
LOOK HARDER
COO-EE!

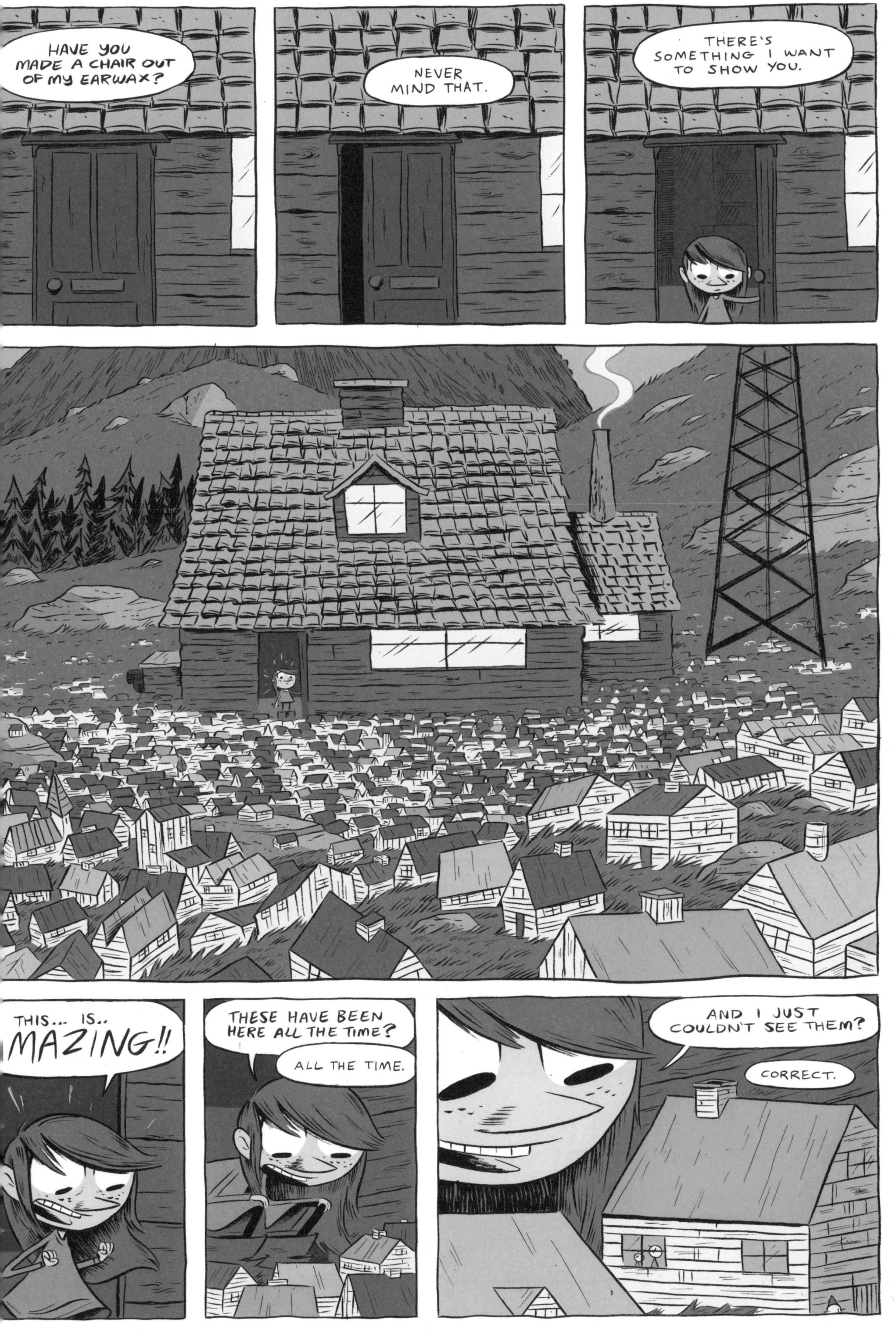
HAVE YOU MADE A CHAIR OUT OF MY EARWAX?
NEVER MIND THAT.
THERE'S SOMETHING I WANT TO SHOW YOU.
THIS... IS.. MAZING!!
THESE HAVE BEEN HERE ALL THE TIME?
ALL THE TIME.
AND I JUST COULDN'T SEE THEM?
CORRECT.

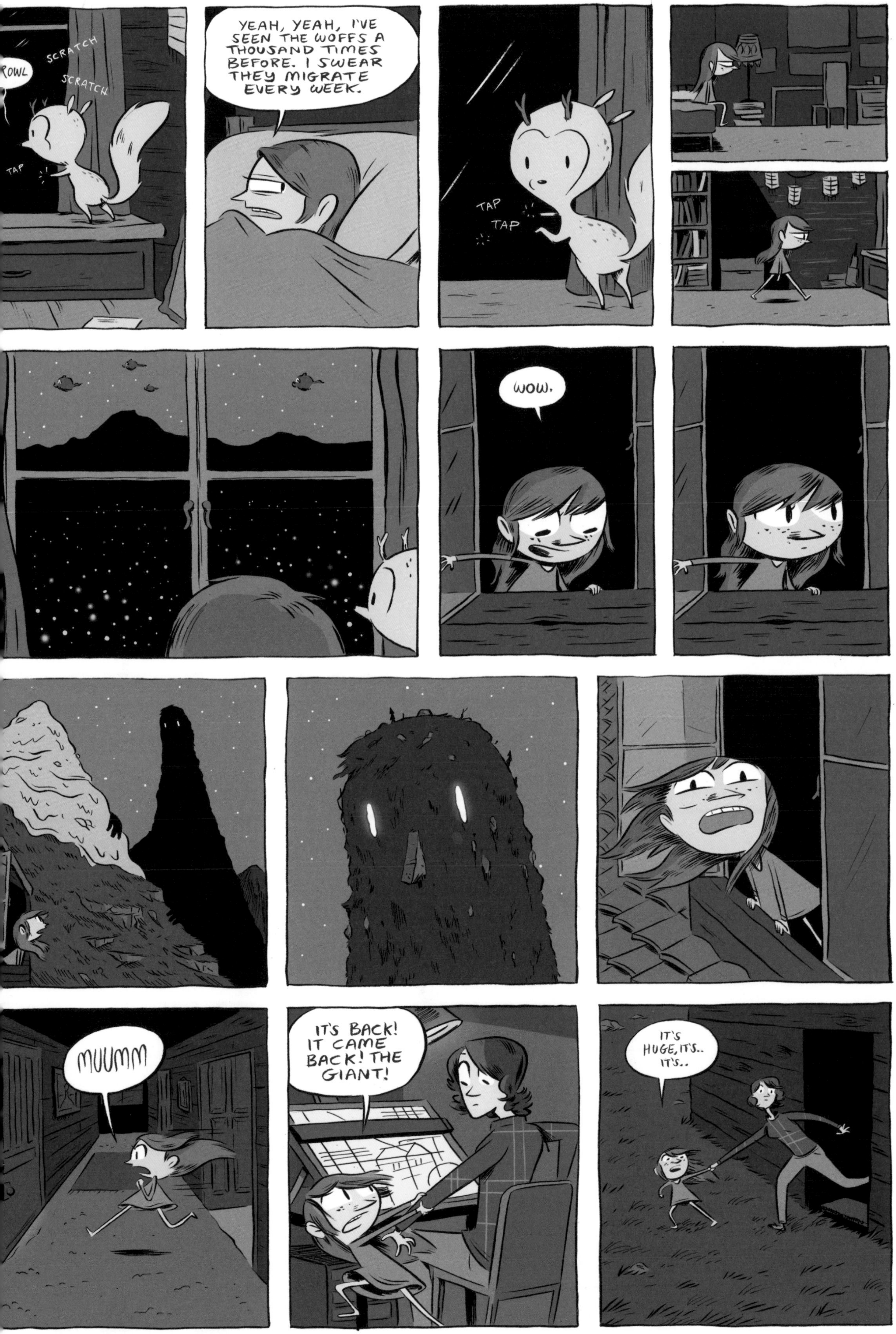
ROWL
SCRATCH
SCRATCH
TAP
YEAH, YEAH, I'VE SEEN THE WOFFS A THOUSAND TIMES BEFORE. I SWEAR THEY MIGRATE EVERY WEEK.
TAP
TAP
WOW.
MUUMM
IT'S BACK! IT CAME BACK! THE GIANT!
IT'S HUGE, IT'S.. IT'S..

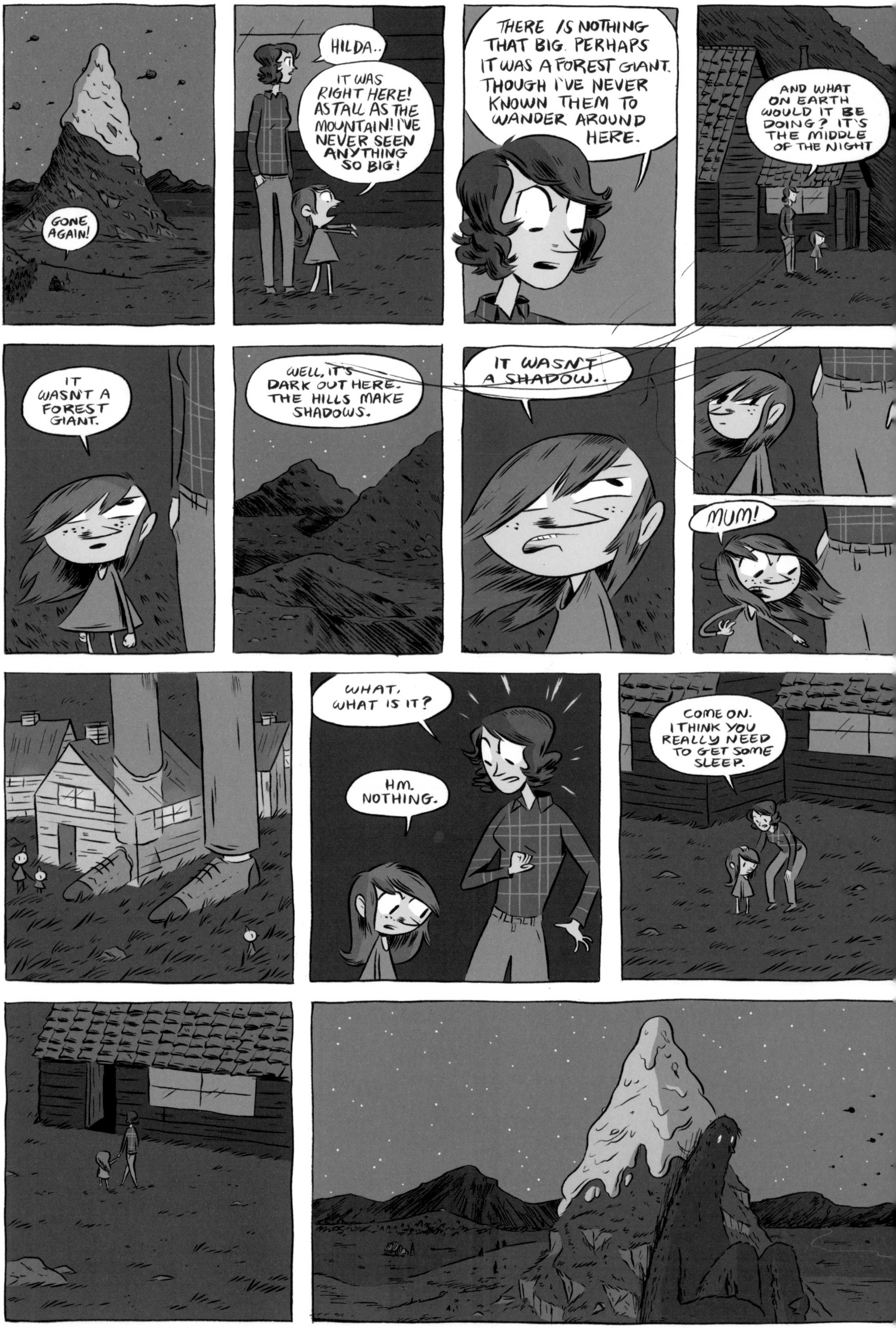
GONE AGAIN!
HILDA..
IT WAS RIGHT HERE! AS TALL AS THE MOUNTAIN! I'VE NEVER SEEN ANYTHING SO BIG!
THERE IS NOTHING THAT BIG. PERHAPS IT WAS A FOREST GIANT. THOUGH I'VE NEVER KNOWN THEM TO WANDER AROUND HERE.
AND WHAT ON EARTH WOULD IT BE DOING? IT'S THE MIDDLE OF THE NIGHT
IT WASN'T A FOREST GIANT.
WELL, IT'S DARK OUT HERE. THE HILLS MAKE SHADOWS.
IT WASN'T A SHADOW..
MUM!
WHAT, WHAT IS IT?
HM. NOTHING.
COME ON. I THINK YOU REALLY NEED TO GET SOME SLEEP.

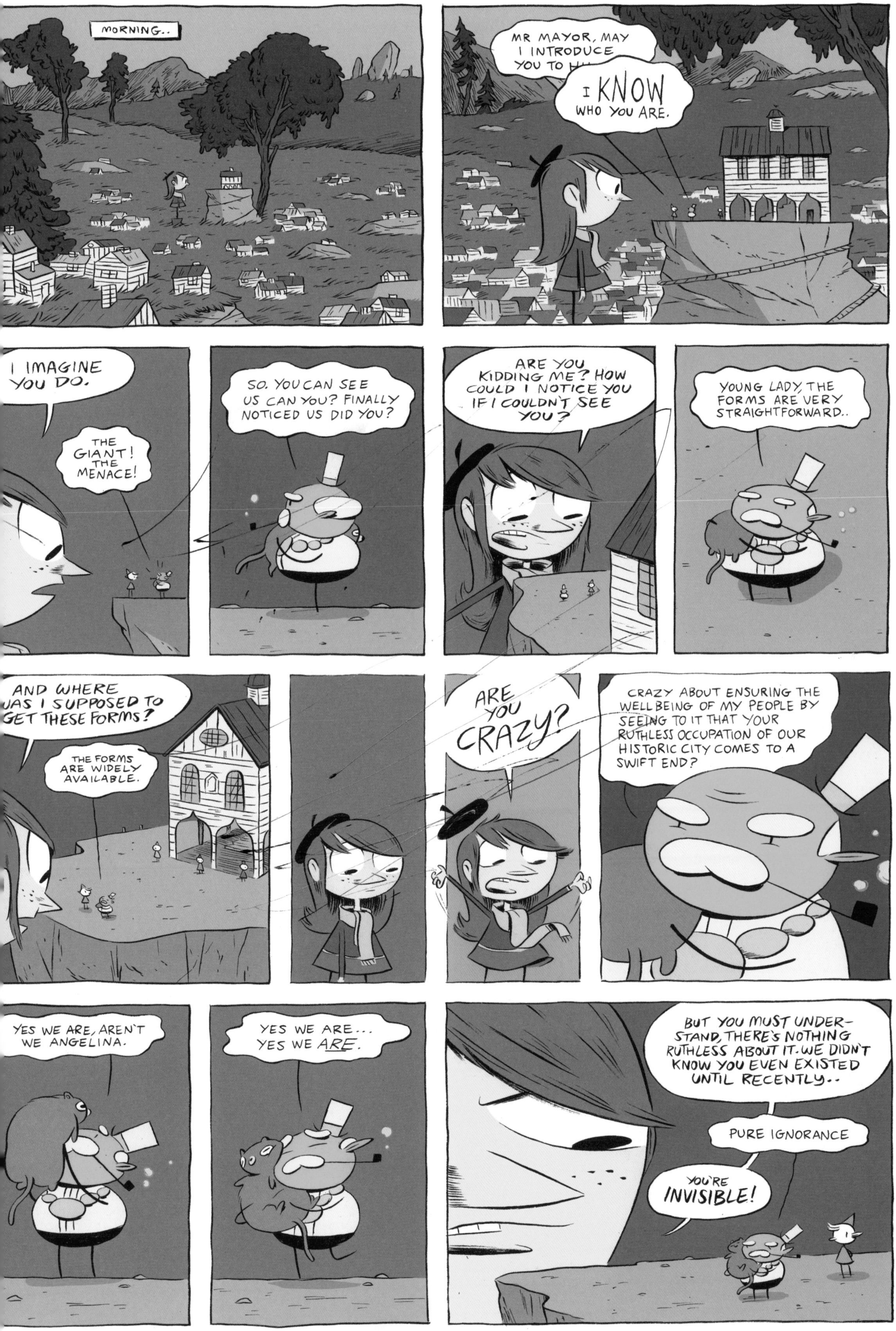
MORNING..
MR MAYOR, MAY I INTRODUCE YOU TO HI
I KNOW WHO YOU ARE.
I IMAGINE YOU DO.
THE GIANT! THE MENACE!
SO. YOU CAN SEE US CAN YOU? FINALLY NOTICED US DID YOU?
ARE YOU KIDDING ME? HOW COULD I NOTICE YOU IF I COULDN'T SEE YOU?
YOUNG LADY, THE FORMS ARE VERY STRAIGHTFORWARD..
AND WHERE WAS I SUPPOSED TO GET THESE FORMS?
THE FORMS ARE WIDELY AVAILABLE.
ARE YOU CRAZY?
CRAZY ABOUT ENSURING THE WELL BEING OF MY PEOPLE BY SEEING TO IT THAT YOUR RUTHLESS OCCUPATION OF OUR HISTORIC CITY COMES TO A SWIFT END?
YES WE ARE, AREN'T WE ANGELINA.
YES WE ARE... YES WE ARE.
BUT YOU MUST UNDERSTAND, THERE'S NOTHING RUTHLESS ABOUT IT. WE DIDN'T KNOW YOU EVEN EXISTED UNTIL RECENTLY..
PURE IGNORANCE
YOU'RE INVISIBLE!

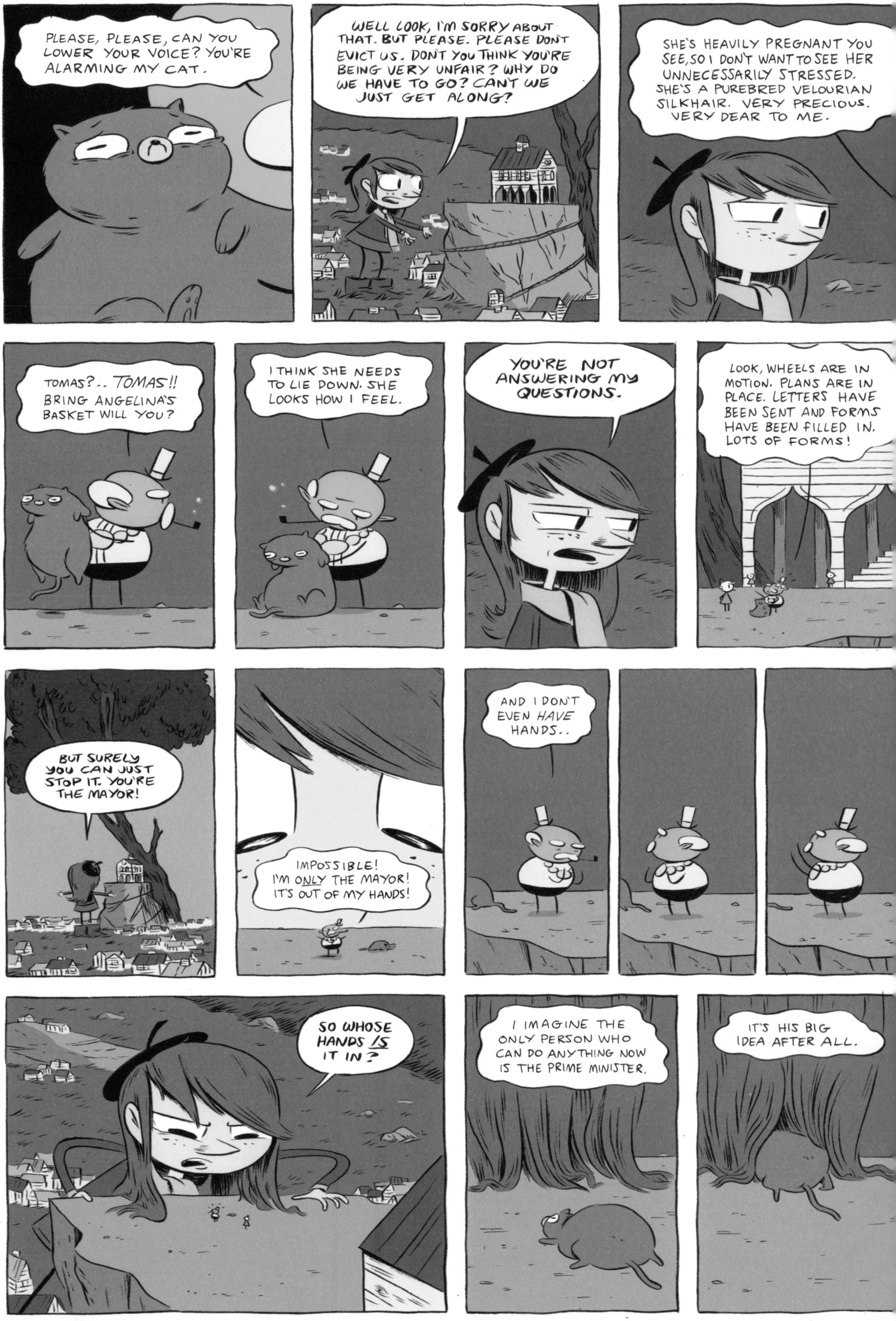
PLEASE, PLEASE, CAN YOU LOWER YOUR VOICE? YOU'RE ALARMING MY CAT.
WELL LOOK, I'M SORRY ABOUT THAT. BUT PLEASE. PLEASE DON'T EVICT US. DON'T YOU THINK YOU'RE BEING VERY UNFAIR? WHY DO WE HAVE TO GO? CAN'T WE JUST GET ALONG?
SHE'S HEAVILY PREGNANT YOU SEE, SO I DON'T WANT TO SEE HER UNNECESSARILY STRESSED. SHE'S A PUREBRED VELOURIAN SILKHAIR. VERY PRECIOUS. VERY DEAR TO ME.
TOMAS?.. TOMAS!! BRING ANGELINA'S BASKET WILL YOU?
I THINK SHE NEEDS TO LIE DOWN. SHE LOOKS HOW I FEEL.
YOU'RE NOT ANSWERING MY QUESTIONS.
LOOK, WHEELS ARE IN MOTION. PLANS ARE IN PLACE. LETTERS HAVE BEEN SENT AND FORMS HAVE BEEN FILLED IN. LOTS OF FORMS!
BUT SURELY YOU CAN JUST STOP IT. YOU'RE THE MAYOR!
IMPOSSIBLE! I'M ONLY THE MAYOR! IT'S OUT OF MY HANDS!
AND I DON'T EVEN HAVE HANDS..
SO WHOSE HANDS IS IT IN?
I IMAGINE THE ONLY PERSON WHO CAN DO ANYTHING NOW IS THE PRIME MINISTER.
IT'S HIS BIG IDEA AFTER ALL.

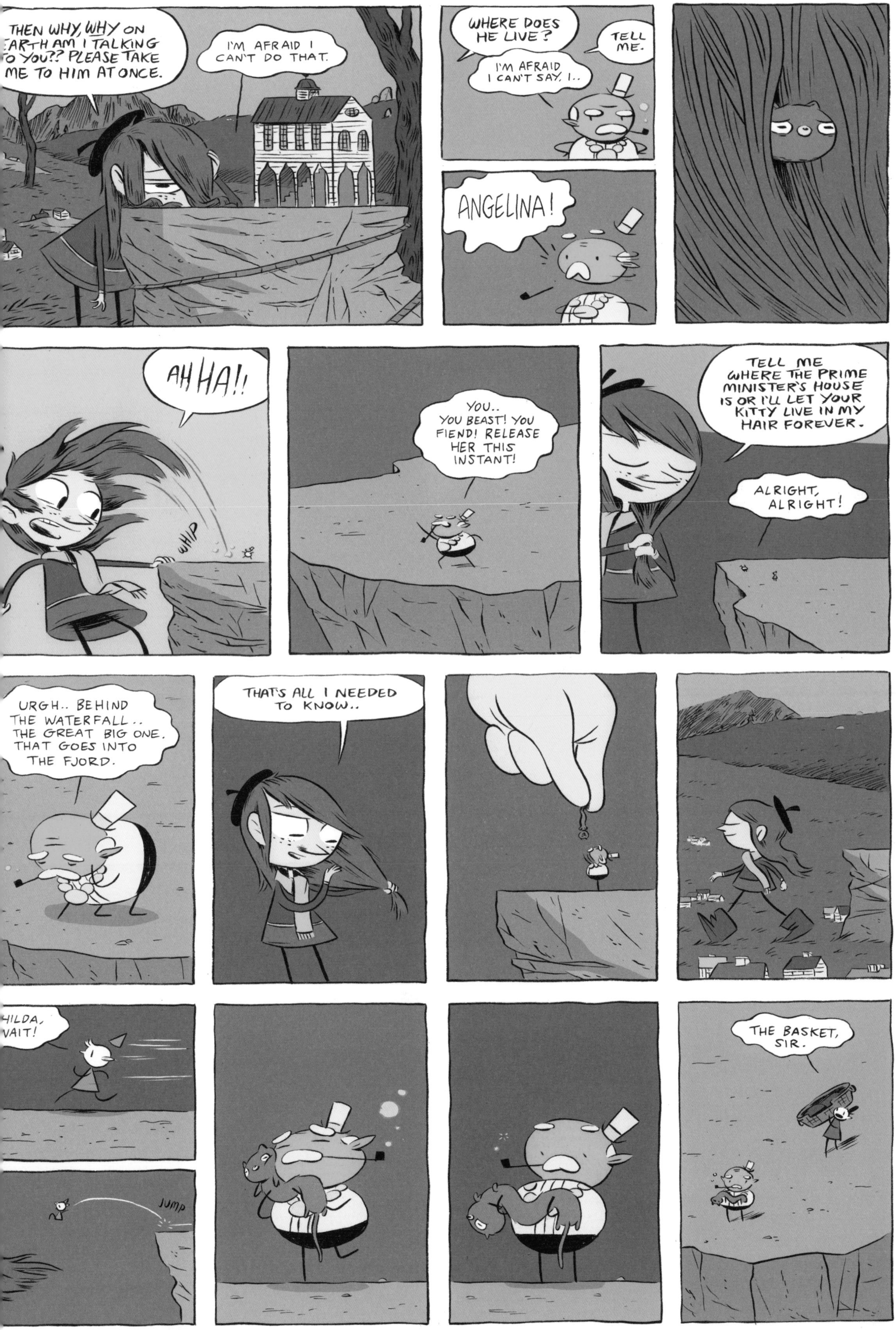
THEN WHY, WHY ON EARTH AM I TALKING TO YOU?? PLEASE TAKE ME TO HIM AT ONCE.
I'M AFRAID I CAN'T DO THAT.
WHERE DOES HE LIVE?
TELL ME.
I'M AFRAID I CAN'T SAY, I..
ANGELINA!
AH HA!!
WHIP
YOU.. YOU BEAST! YOU FIEND! RELEASE HER THIS INSTANT!
TELL ME WHERE THE PRIME MINISTER'S HOUSE IS OR I'LL LET YOUR KITTY LIVE IN MY HAIR FOREVER.
ALRIGHT, ALRIGHT!
URGH.. BEHIND THE WATERFALL.. THE GREAT BIG ONE. THAT GOES INTO THE FJORD.
THAT'S ALL I NEEDED TO KNOW..
HILDA, WAIT!
JUMP
THE BASKET, SIR.

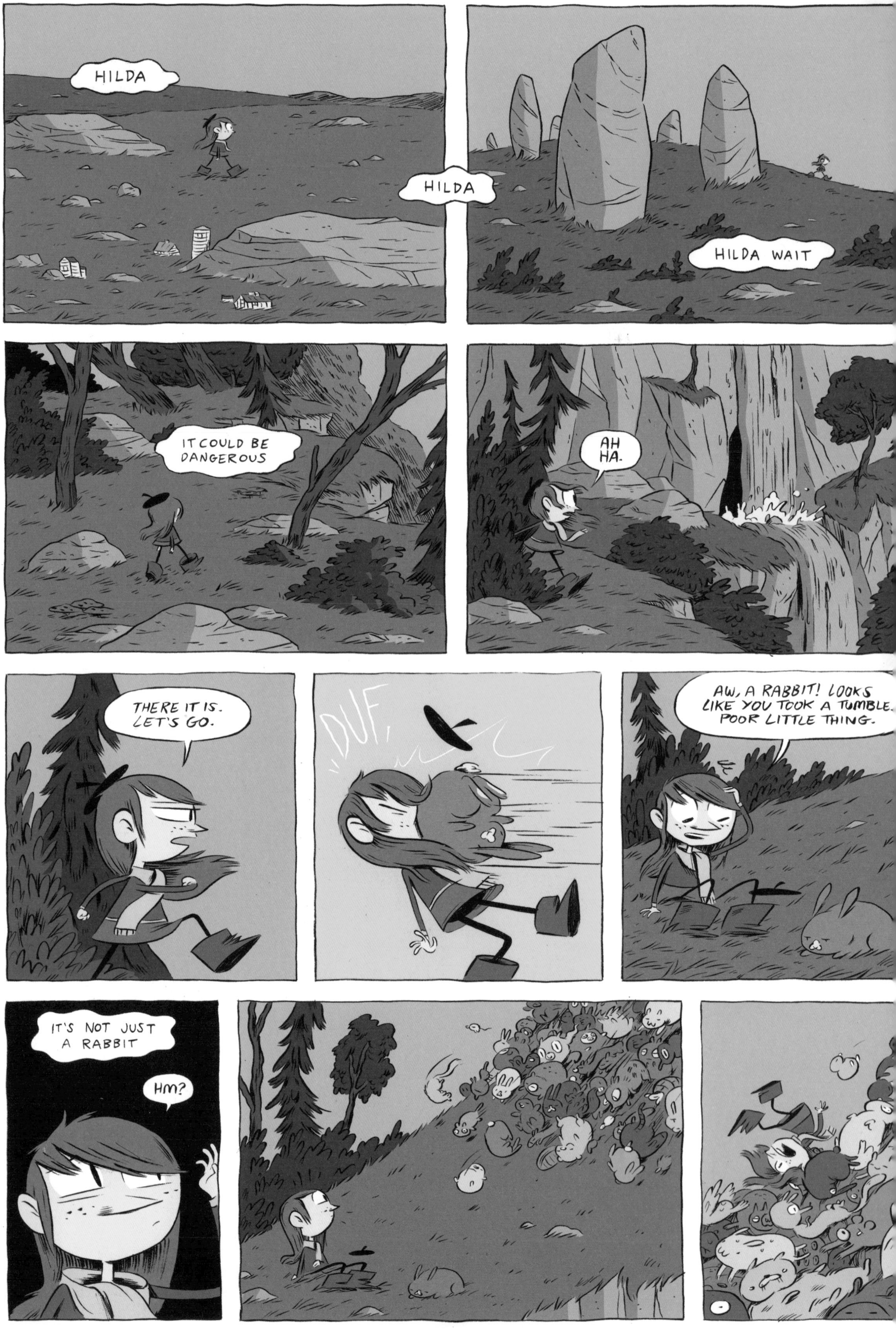
HILDA
HILDA
HILDA WAIT
IT COULD BE DANGEROUS
AH HA.
THERE IT IS. LET'S GO.
DUF,
AW, A RABBIT! LOOKS LIKE YOU TOOK A TUMBLE. POOR LITTLE THING.
IT'S NOT JUST A RABBIT
HM?

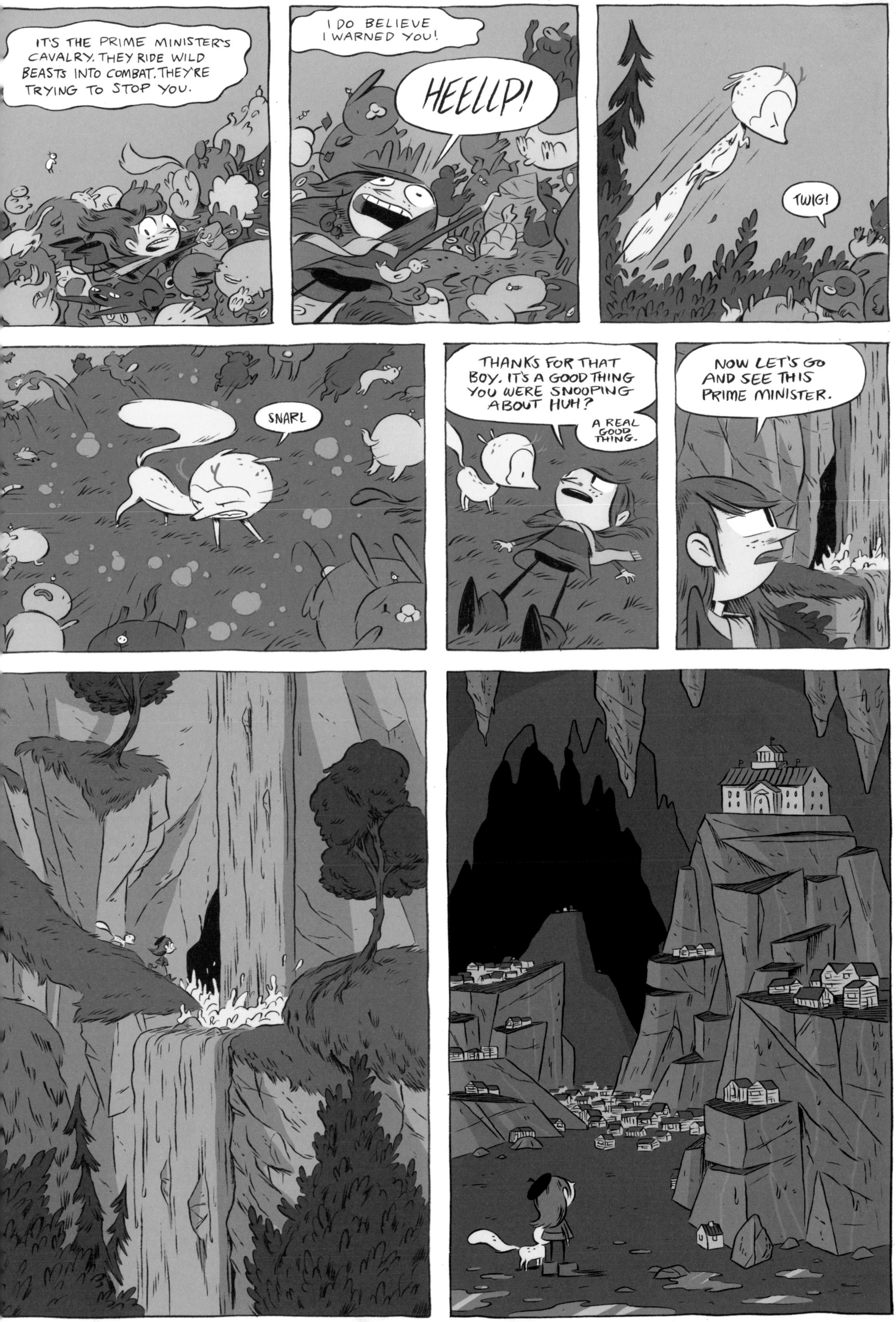
IT'S THE PRIME MINISTER'S CAVALRY. THEY RIDE WILD BEASTS INTO COMBAT. THEY'RE TRYING TO STOP YOU.
I DO BELIEVE I WARNED YOU!
HEELLP!
TWIG!
SNARL
THANKS FOR THAT BOY. IT'S A GOOD THING YOU WERE SNOOPING ABOUT HUH?
A REAL GOOD THING.
NOW LET'S GO AND SEE THIS PRIME MINISTER.

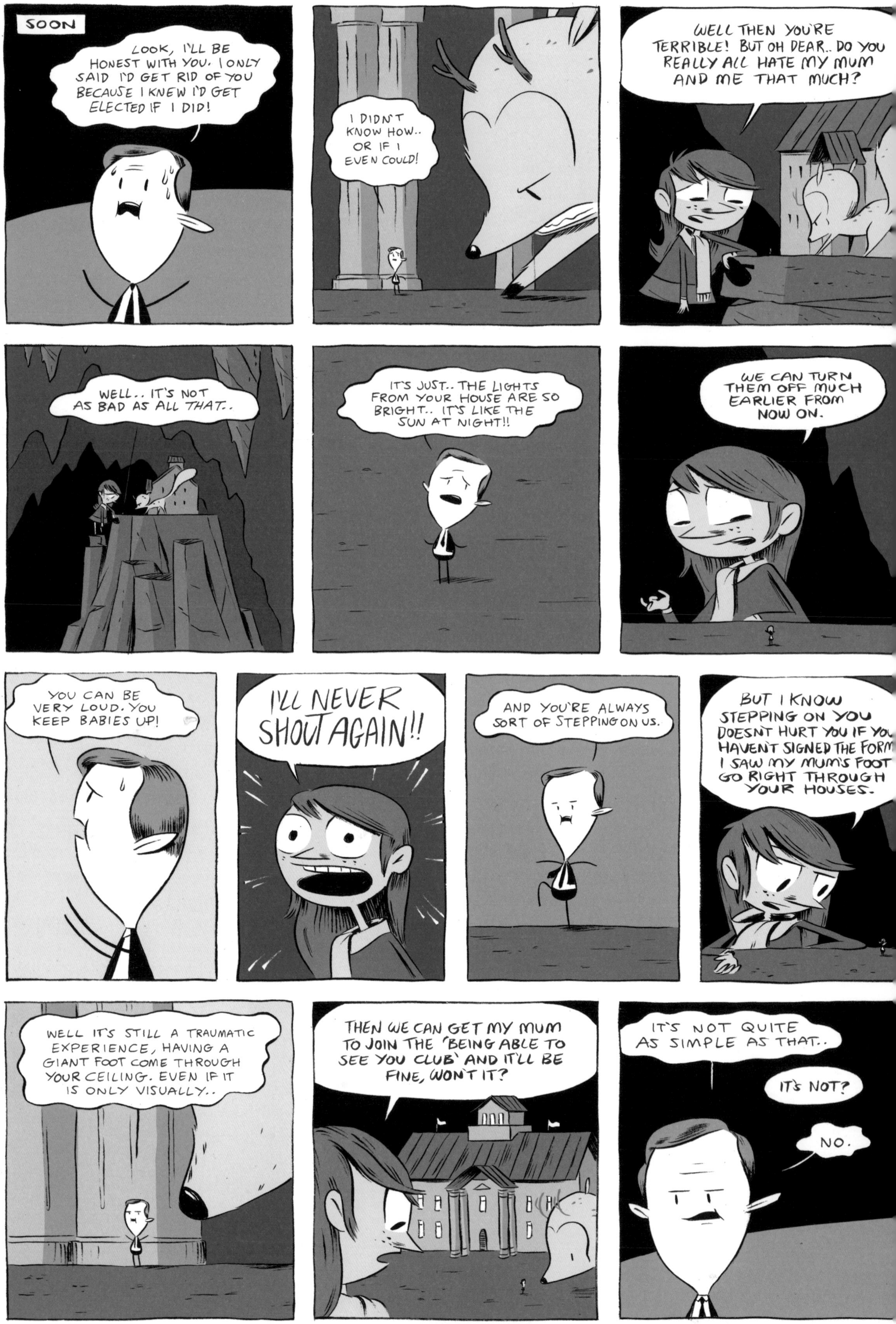
SOON
LOOK, I'LL BE HONEST WITH YOU. I ONLY SAID I'D GET RID OF YOU BECAUSE I KNEW I'D GET ELECTED IF I DID!
I DIDN'T KNOW HOW.. OR IF I EVEN COULD!
WELL THEN YOU'RE TERRIBLE! BUT OH DEAR.. DO YOU REALLY ALL HATE MY MUM AND ME THAT MUCH?
WELL.. IT'S NOT AS BAD AS ALL THAT..
IT'S JUST.. THE LIGHTS FROM YOUR HOUSE ARE SO BRIGHT.. IT'S LIKE THE SUN AT NIGHT!!
WE CAN TURN THEM OFF MUCH EARLIER FROM NOW ON.
YOU CAN BE VERY LOUD. YOU KEEP BABIES UP!
I'LL NEVER SHOUT AGAIN!!
AND YOU'RE ALWAYS SORT OF STEPPING ON US.
BUT I KNOW STEPPING ON YOU DOESN'T HURT YOU IF YOU HAVEN'T SIGNED THE FORM I SAW MY MUM'S FOOT GO RIGHT THROUGH YOUR HOUSES.
WELL IT'S STILL A TRAUMATIC EXPERIENCE, HAVING A GIANT FOOT COME THROUGH YOUR CEILING. EVEN IF IT IS ONLY VISUALLY..
THEN WE CAN GET MY MUM TO JOIN THE 'BEING ABLE TO SEE YOU CLUB' AND IT'LL BE FINE, WON'T IT?
IT'S NOT QUITE AS SIMPLE AS THAT..
IT'S NOT?
NO.

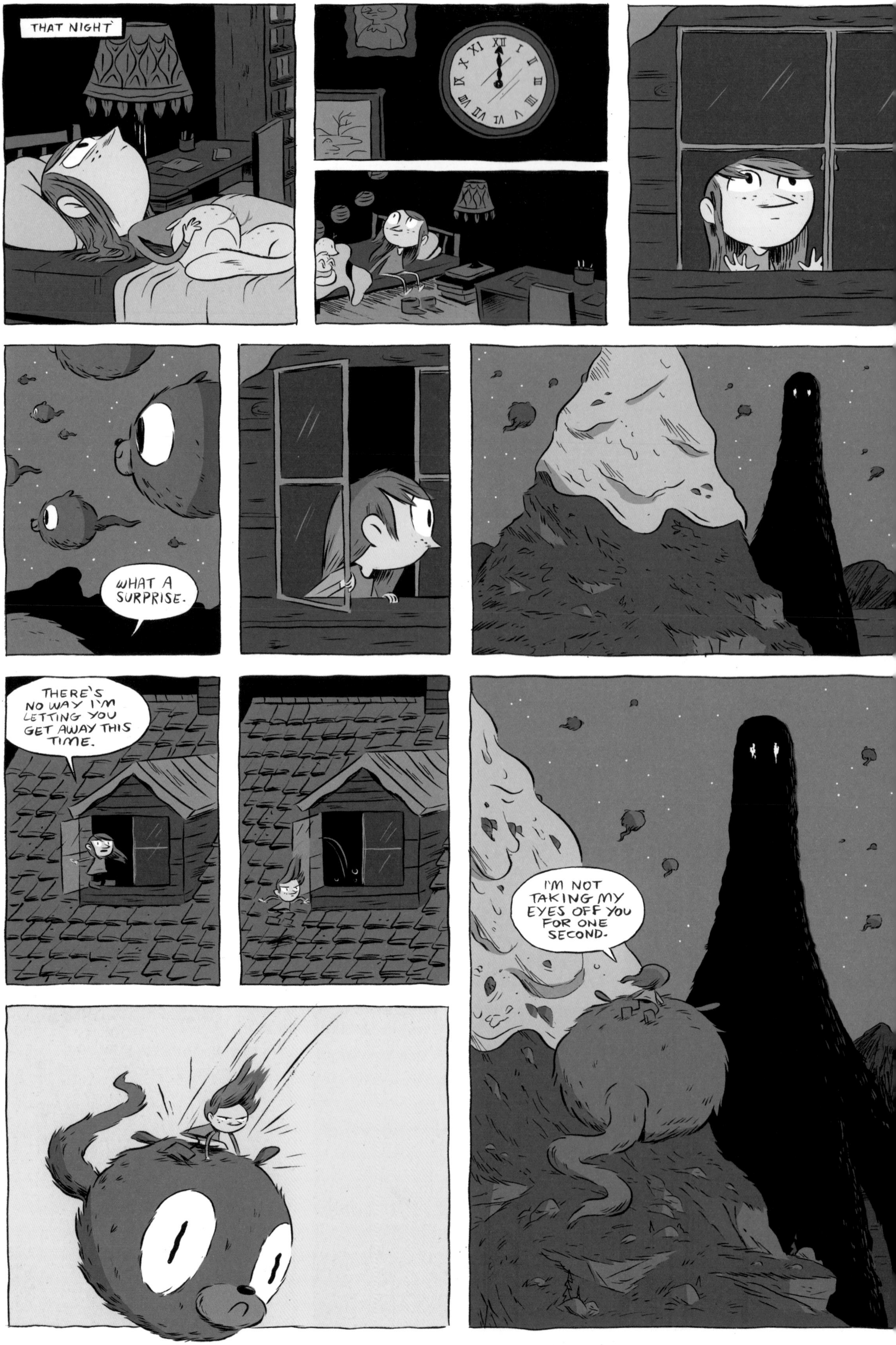
THAT NIGHT
WHAT A SURPRISE.
THERE'S NO WAY I'M LETTING YOU GET AWAY THIS TIME.
I'M NOT TAKING MY EYES OFF YOU FOR ONE SECOND.

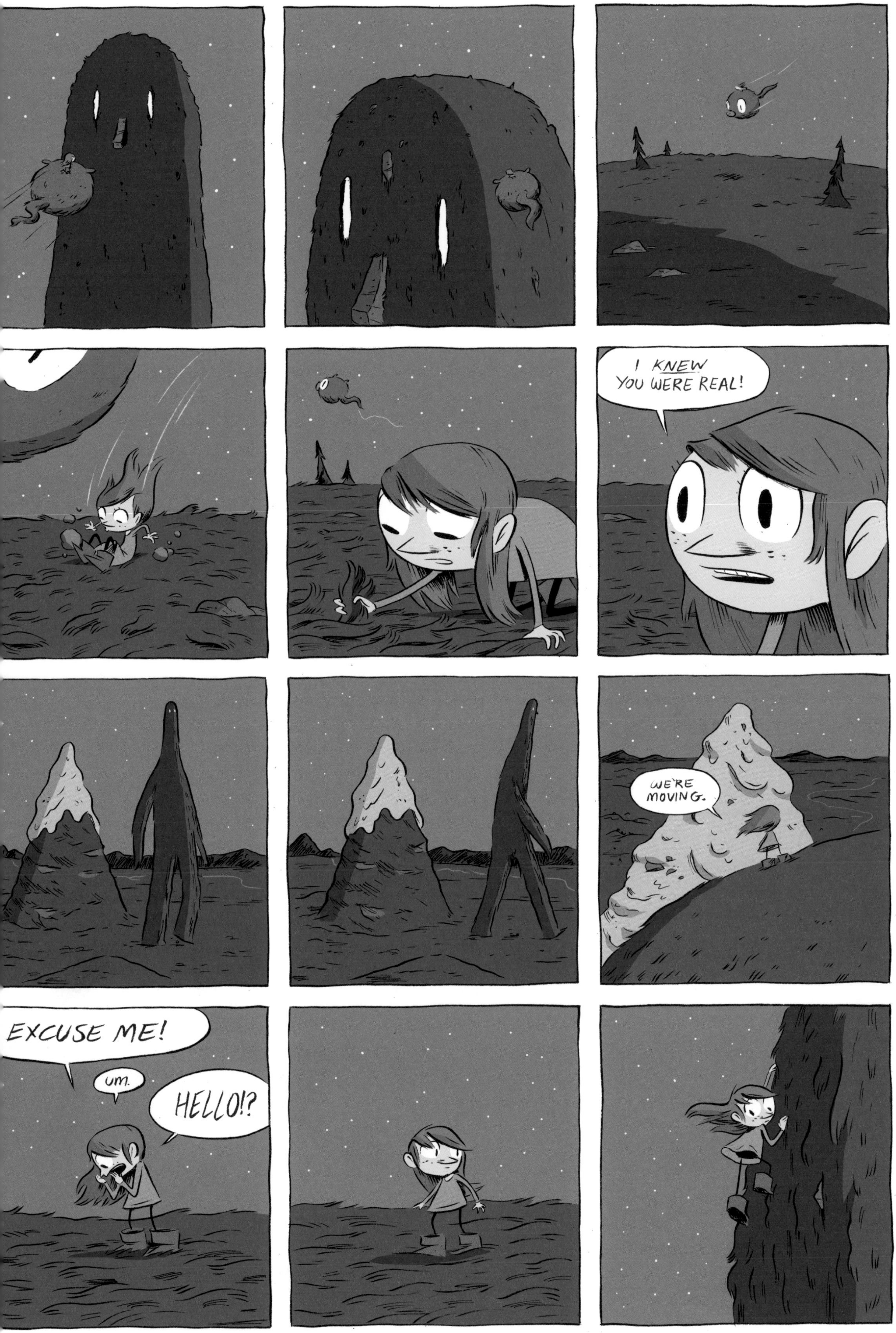

I KNEW YOU WERE REAL!
WE'RE MOVING.
EXCUSE ME!
um.
HELLO!?

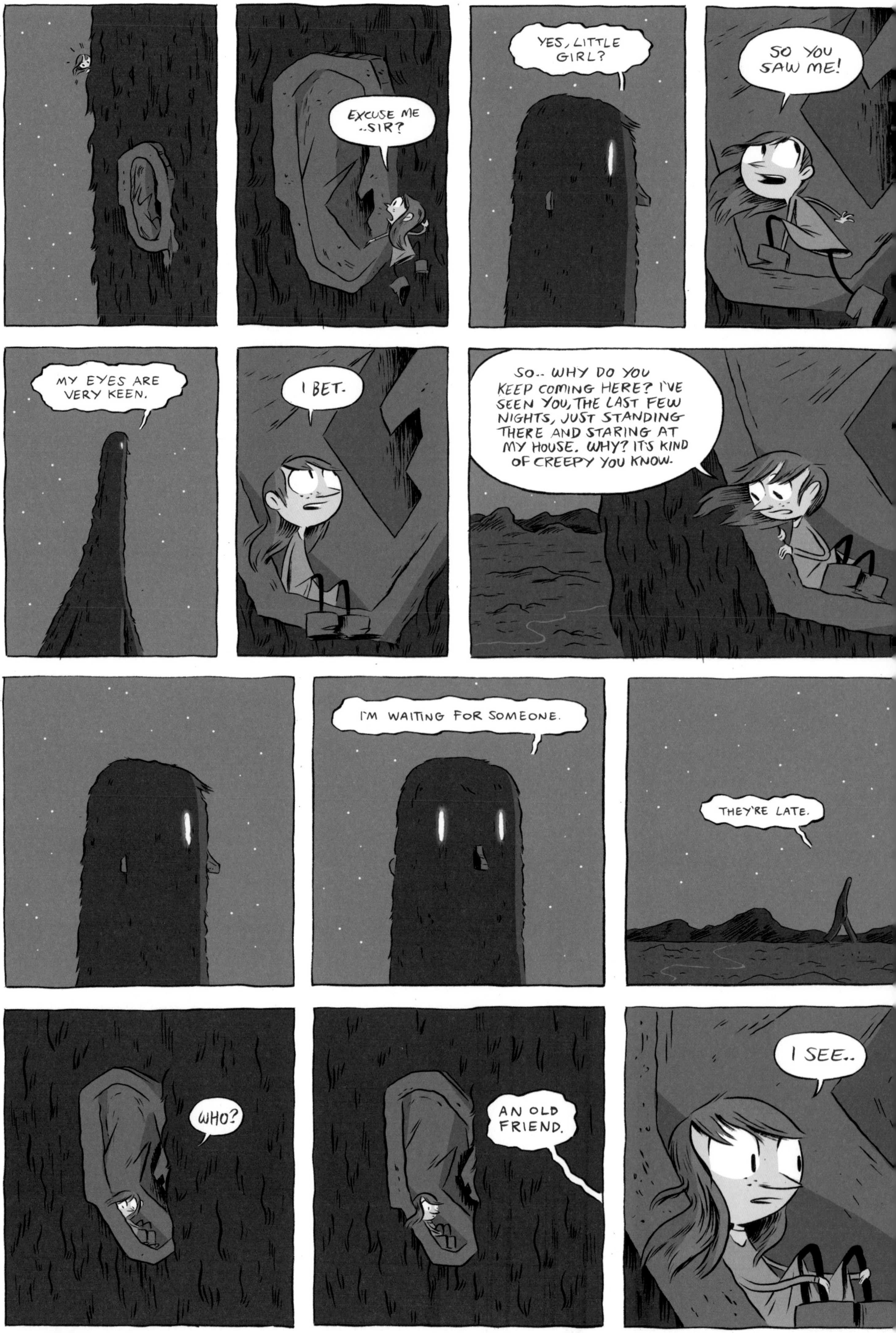
EXCUSE ME
..SIR?
YES, LITTLE
GIRL?
SO YOU
SAW ME!
MY EYES ARE
VERY KEEN.
I BET.
SO.. WHY DO YOU KEEP COMING HERE? I'VE SEEN YOU, THE LAST FEW NIGHTS, JUST STANDING THERE AND STARING AT MY HOUSE. WHY? IT'S KIND OF CREEPY YOU KNOW.
I'M WAITING FOR SOMEONE.
THEY'RE LATE.
WHO?
AN OLD
FRIEND.
I SEE..

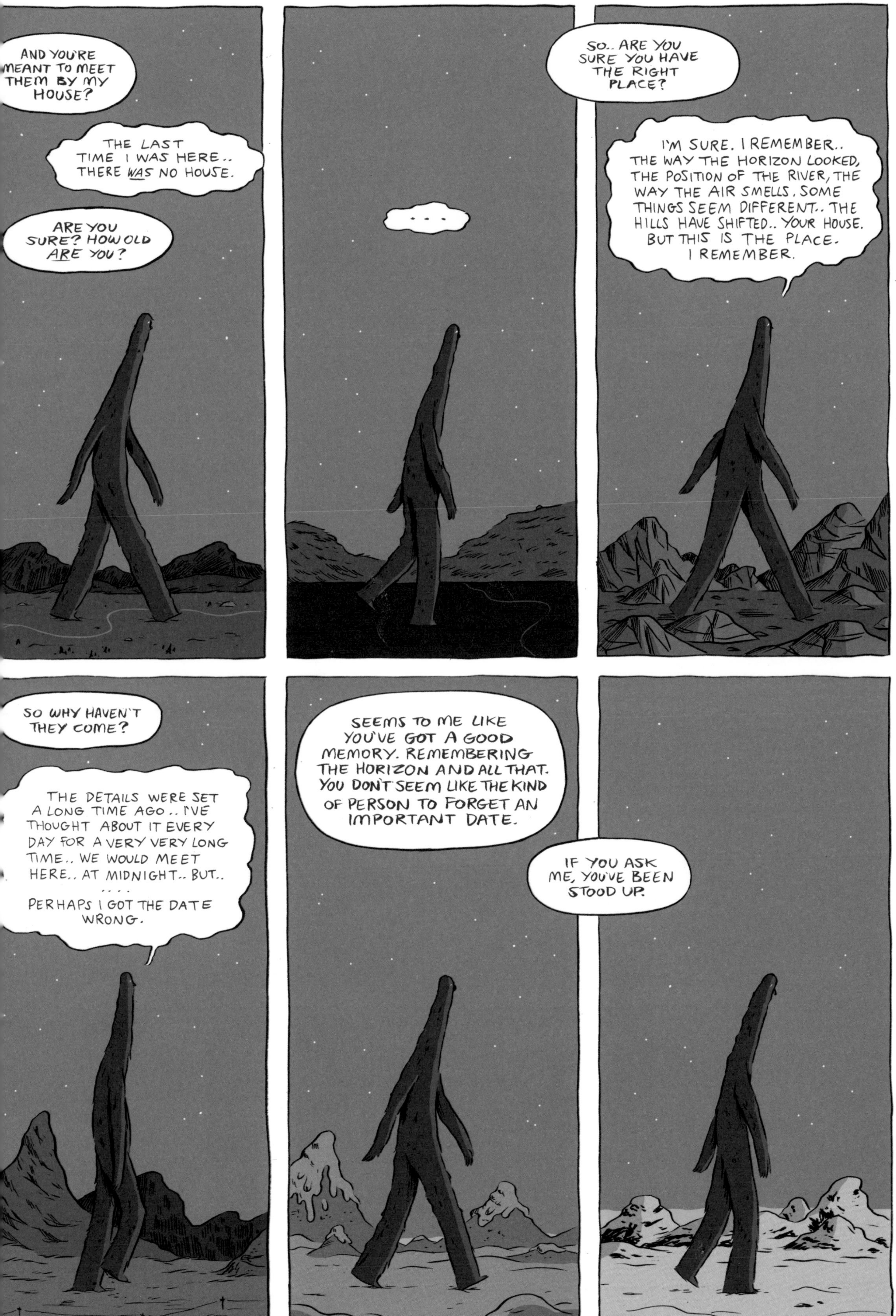
AND YOU'RE MEANT TO MEET THEM BY MY HOUSE?
THE LAST TIME I WAS HERE.. THERE WAS NO HOUSE.
ARE YOU SURE? HOW OLD ARE YOU?
...
SO.. ARE YOU SURE YOU HAVE THE RIGHT PLACE?
I'M SURE. I REMEMBER.. THE WAY THE HORIZON LOOKED, THE POSITION OF THE RIVER, THE WAY THE AIR SMELLS. SOME THINGS SEEM DIFFERENT.. THE HILLS HAVE SHIFTED.. YOUR HOUSE. BUT THIS IS THE PLACE. I REMEMBER.
SO WHY HAVEN'T THEY COME?
THE DETAILS WERE SET A LONG TIME AGO.. I'VE THOUGHT ABOUT IT EVERY DAY FOR A VERY VERY LONG TIME.. WE WOULD MEET HERE.. AT MIDNIGHT.. BUT.. .... PERHAPS I GOT THE DATE WRONG.
SEEMS TO ME LIKE YOU'VE GOT A GOOD MEMORY. REMEMBERING THE HORIZON AND ALL THAT. YOU DON'T SEEM LIKE THE KIND OF PERSON TO FORGET AN IMPORTANT DATE.
IF YOU ASK ME, YOU'VE BEEN STOOD UP.

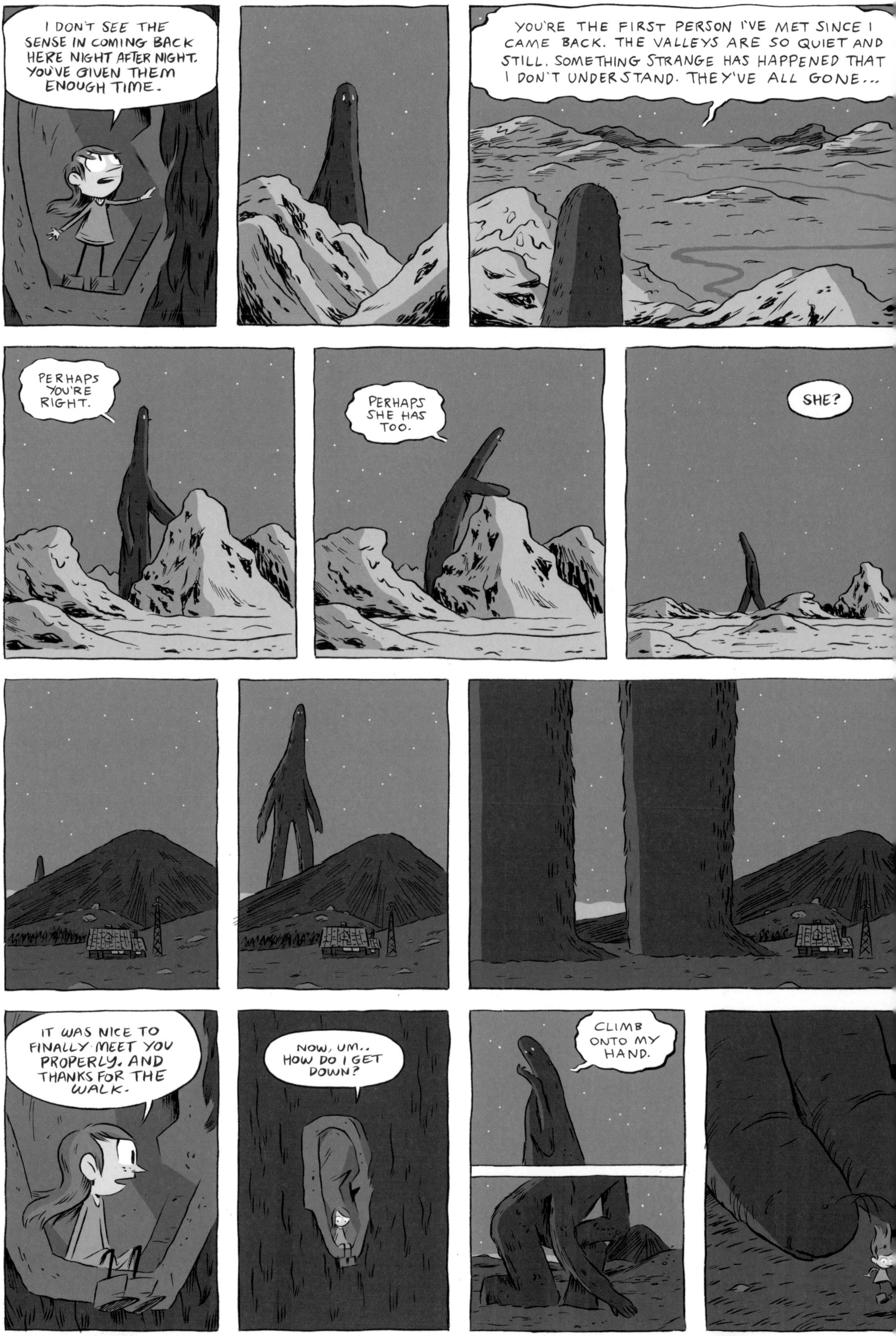
I DON'T SEE THE SENSE IN COMING BACK HERE NIGHT AFTER NIGHT. YOU'VE GIVEN THEM ENOUGH TIME.
YOU'RE THE FIRST PERSON I'VE MET SINCE I CAME BACK. THE VALLEYS ARE SO QUIET AND STILL. SOMETHING STRANGE HAS HAPPENED THAT I DON'T UNDERSTAND. THEY'VE ALL GONE...
PERHAPS YOU'RE RIGHT.
PERHAPS SHE HAS TOO.
SHE?
IT WAS NICE TO FINALLY MEET YOU PROPERLY. AND THANKS FOR THE WALK.
NOW, UM.. HOW DO I GET DOWN?
CLIMB ONTO MY HAND.

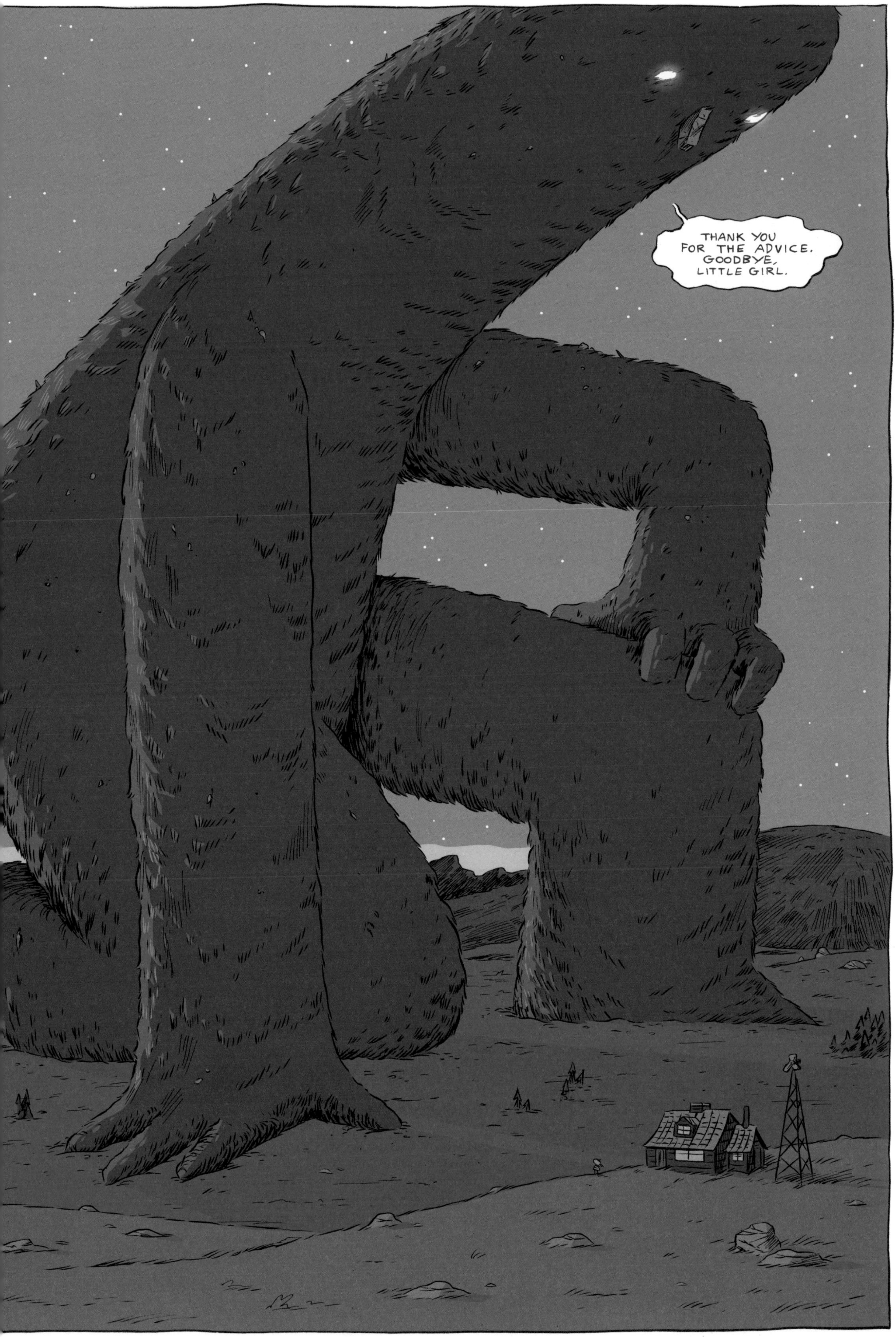
THANK YOU FOR THE ADVICE. GOODBYE, LITTLE GIRL.

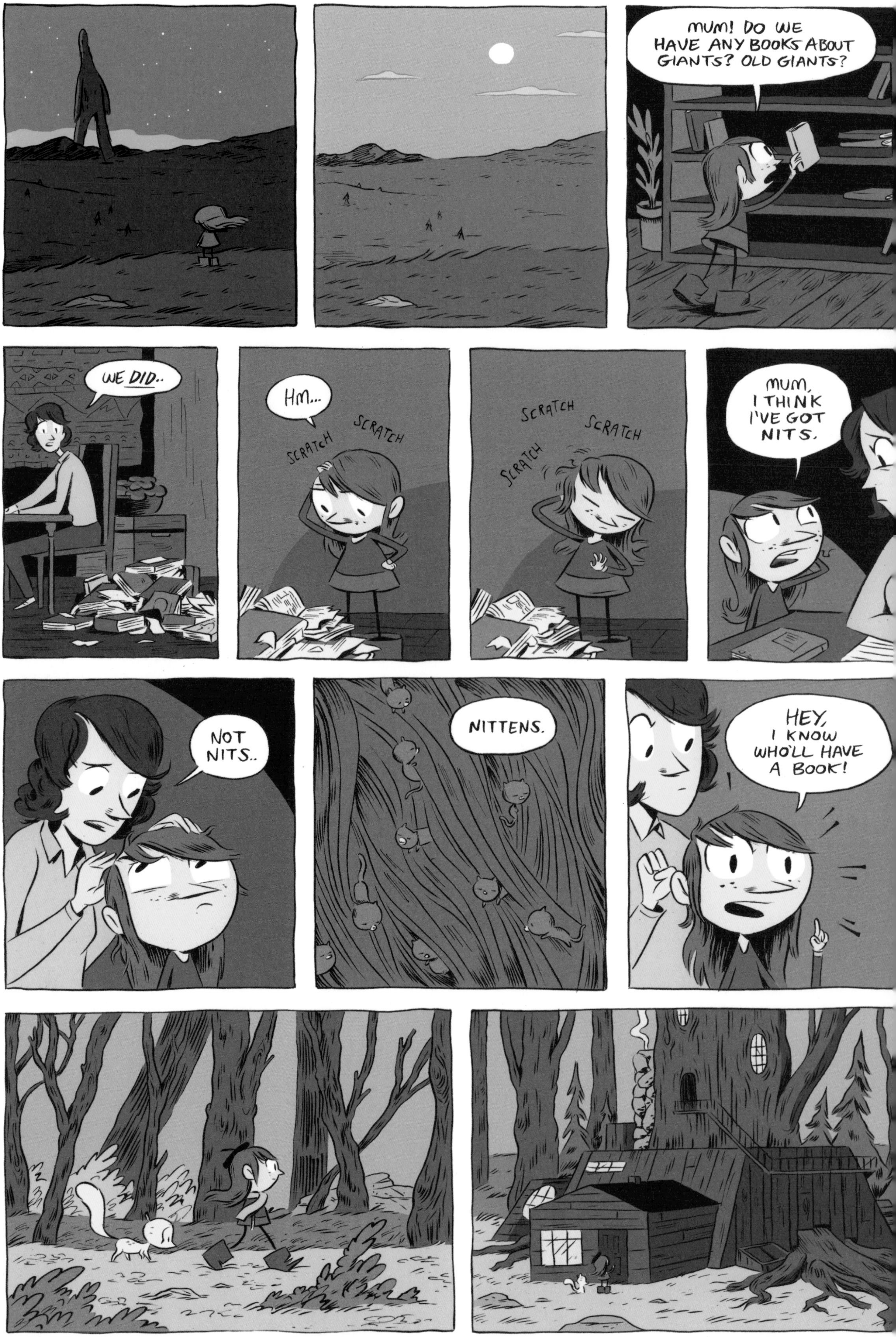
MUM! DO WE HAVE ANY BOOKS ABOUT GIANTS? OLD GIANTS?
WE DID..
HM...
SCRATCH
SCRATCH
SCRATCH
SCRATCH
SCRATCH
MUM, I THINK I'VE GOT NITS.
NOT NITS..
NITTENS.
HEY, I KNOW WHO'LL HAVE A BOOK!

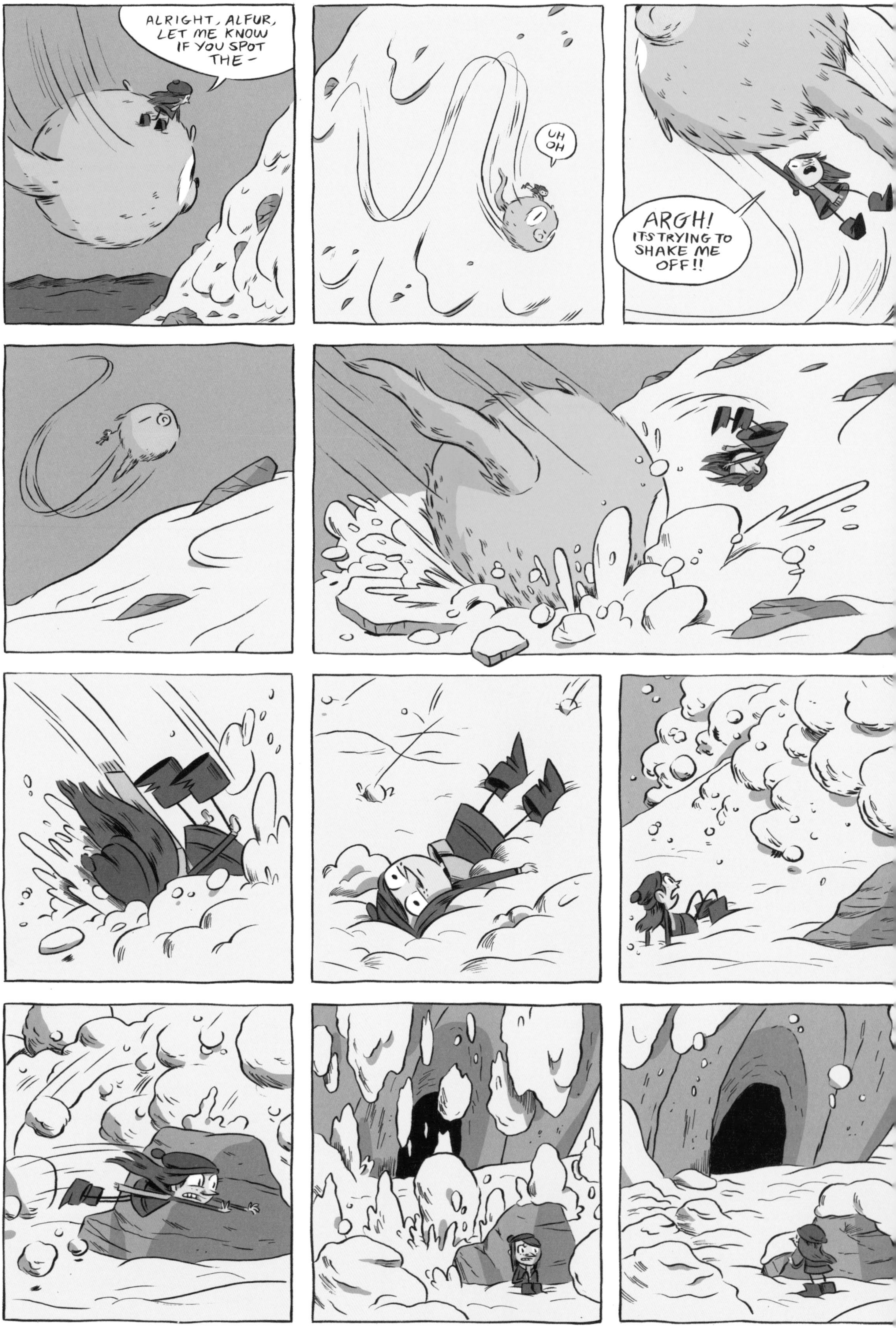
ALRIGHT, ALFUR, LET ME KNOW IF YOU SPOT THE-
UH OH
ARGH! ITS TRYING TO SHAKE ME OFF!!

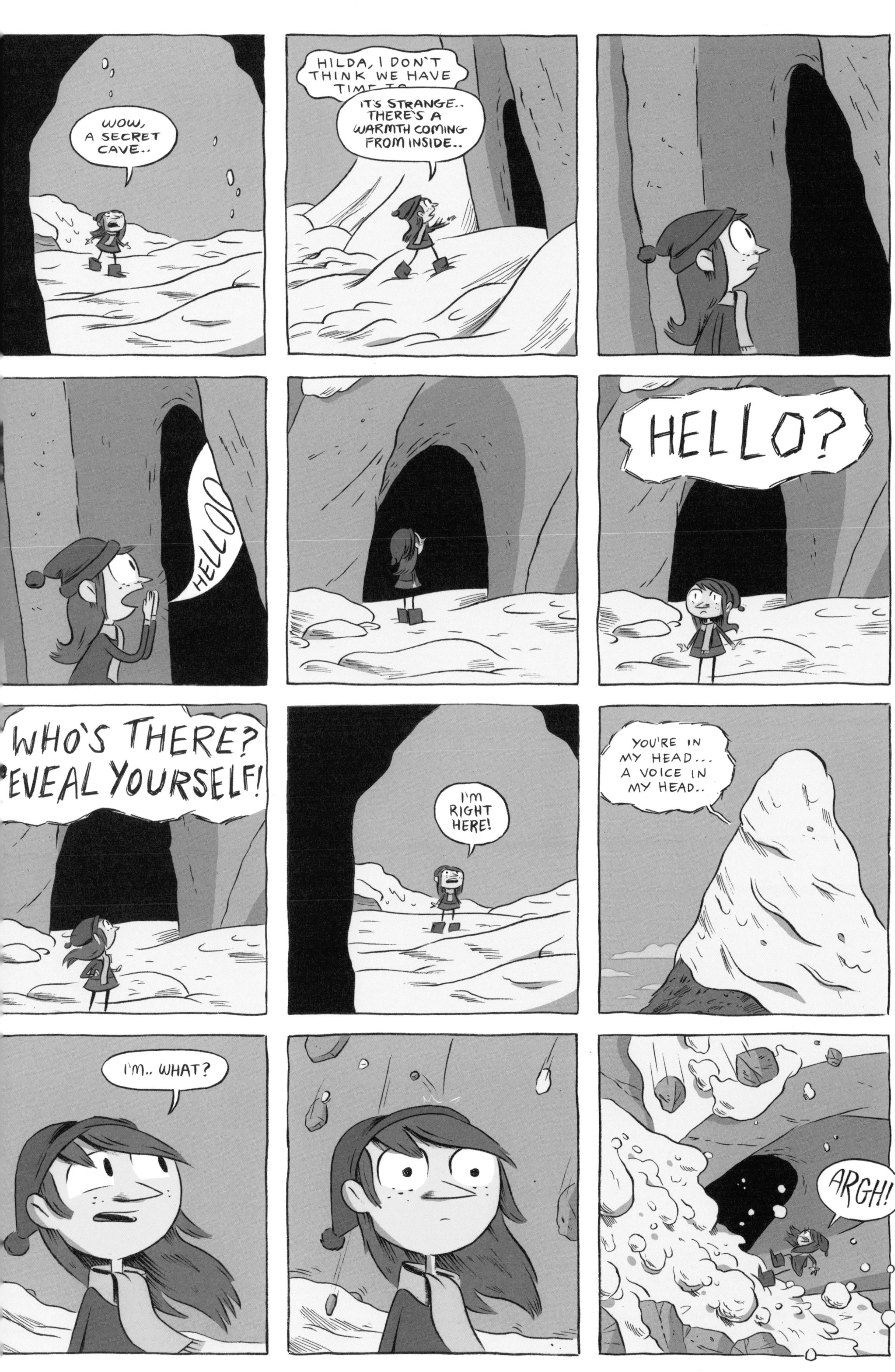
WOW, A SECRET CAVE..
HILDA, I DON'T THINK WE HAVE TIME TO
IT'S STRANGE.. THERE'S A WARMTH COMING FROM INSIDE..
HELLO
HELLO?
WHO'S THERE? EVEAL YOURSELF!
I'M RIGHT HERE!
YOU'RE IN MY HEAD... A VOICE IN MY HEAD..
I'M.. WHAT?
ARGH!

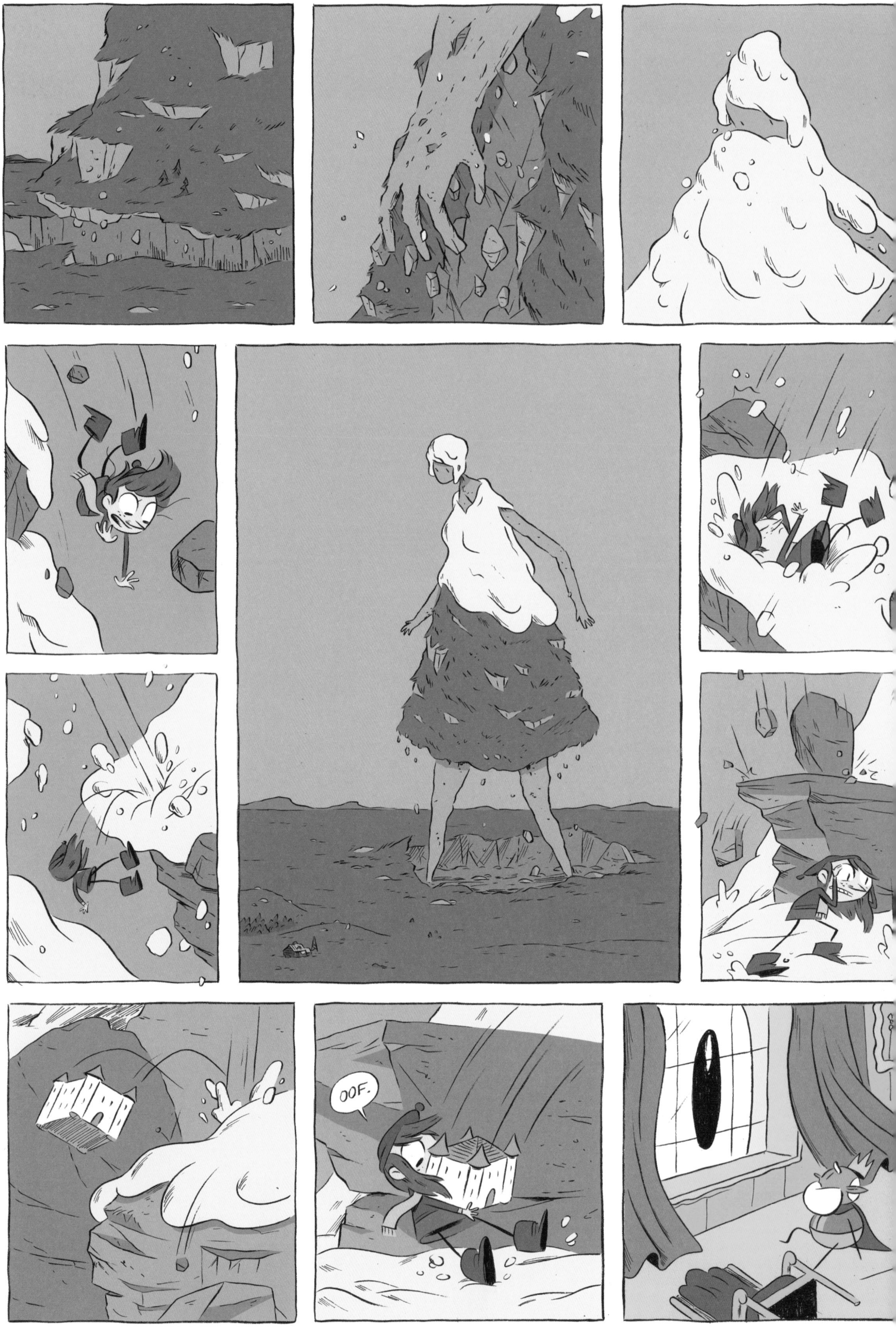
OOF.

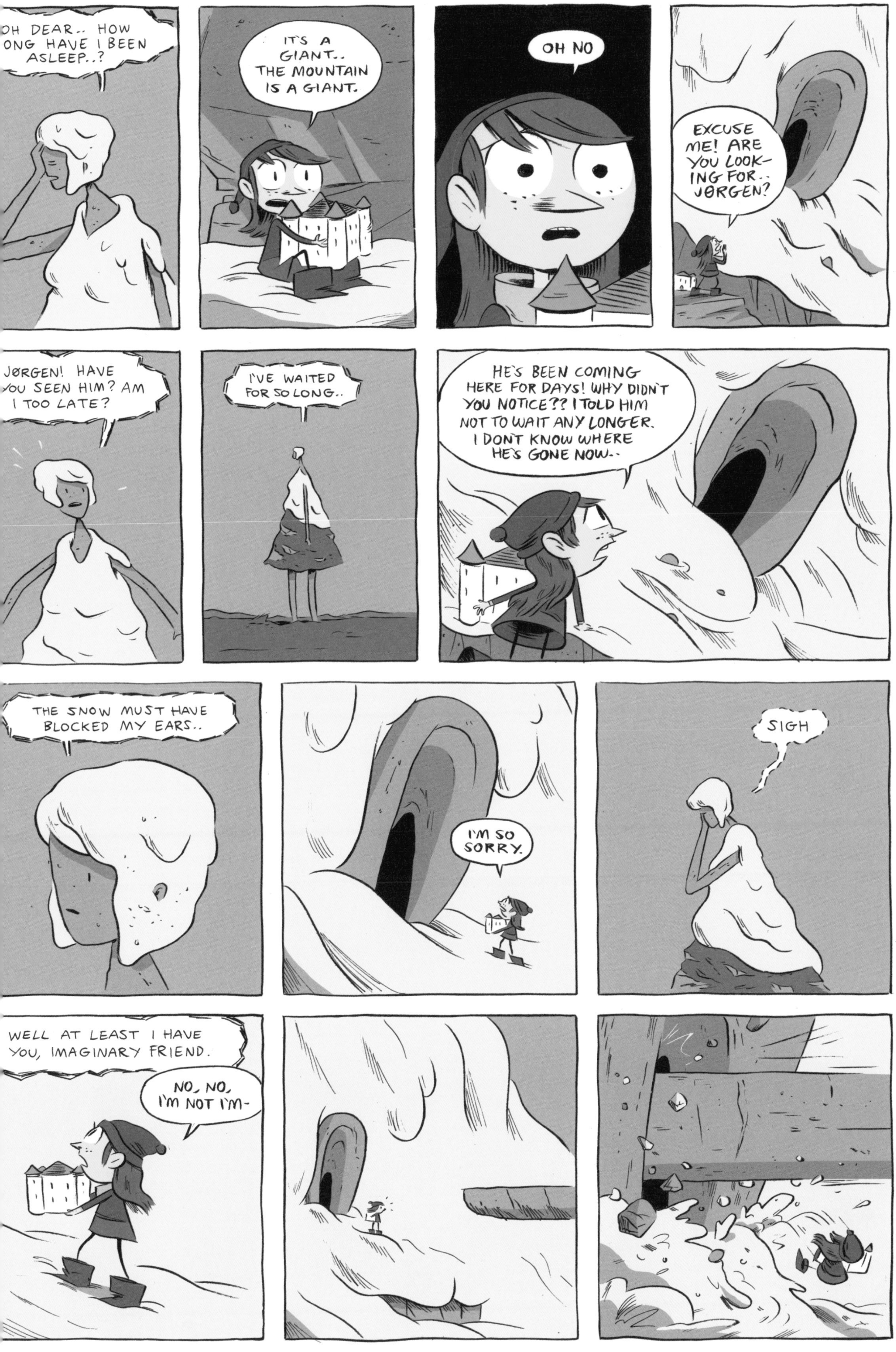
OH DEAR.. HOW
ONG HAVE I BEEN ASLEEP..?
IT'S A GIANT.. THE MOUNTAIN IS A GIANT.
OH NO
EXCUSE ME! ARE YOU LOOKING FOR.. JØRGEN?
JØRGEN! HAVE YOU SEEN HIM? AM I TOO LATE?
I'VE WAITED FOR SO LONG..
HE'S BEEN COMING HERE FOR DAYS! WHY DIDN'T YOU NOTICE?? I TOLD HIM NOT TO WAIT ANY LONGER. I DON'T KNOW WHERE HE'S GONE NOW..
THE SNOW MUST HAVE BLOCKED MY EARS..
I'M SO SORRY.
SIGH
WELL AT LEAST I HAVE YOU, IMAGINARY FRIEND.
NO, NO, I'M NOT I'M-

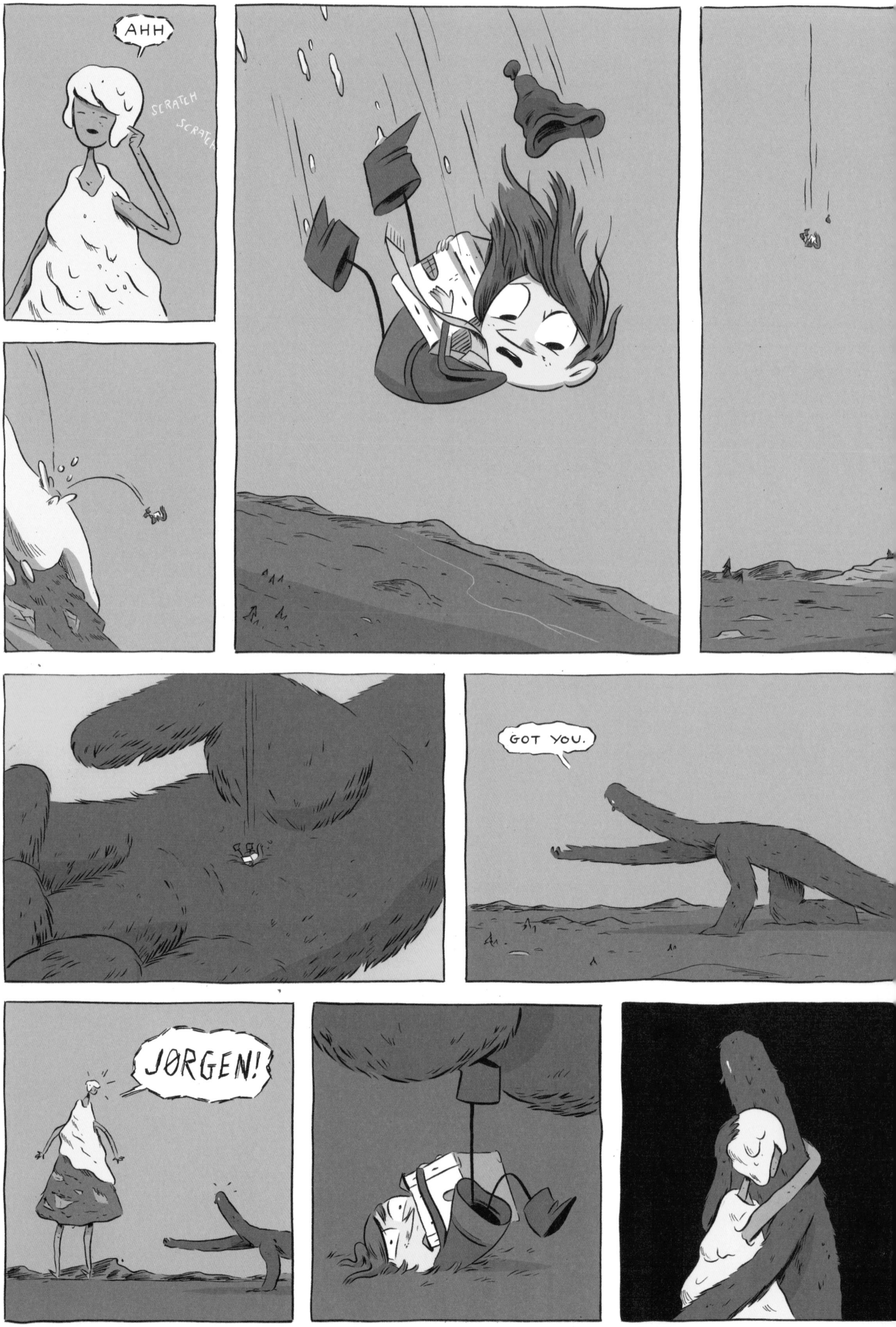
AHH
SCRATCH
SCRATCH
GOT YOU.
JØRGEN!

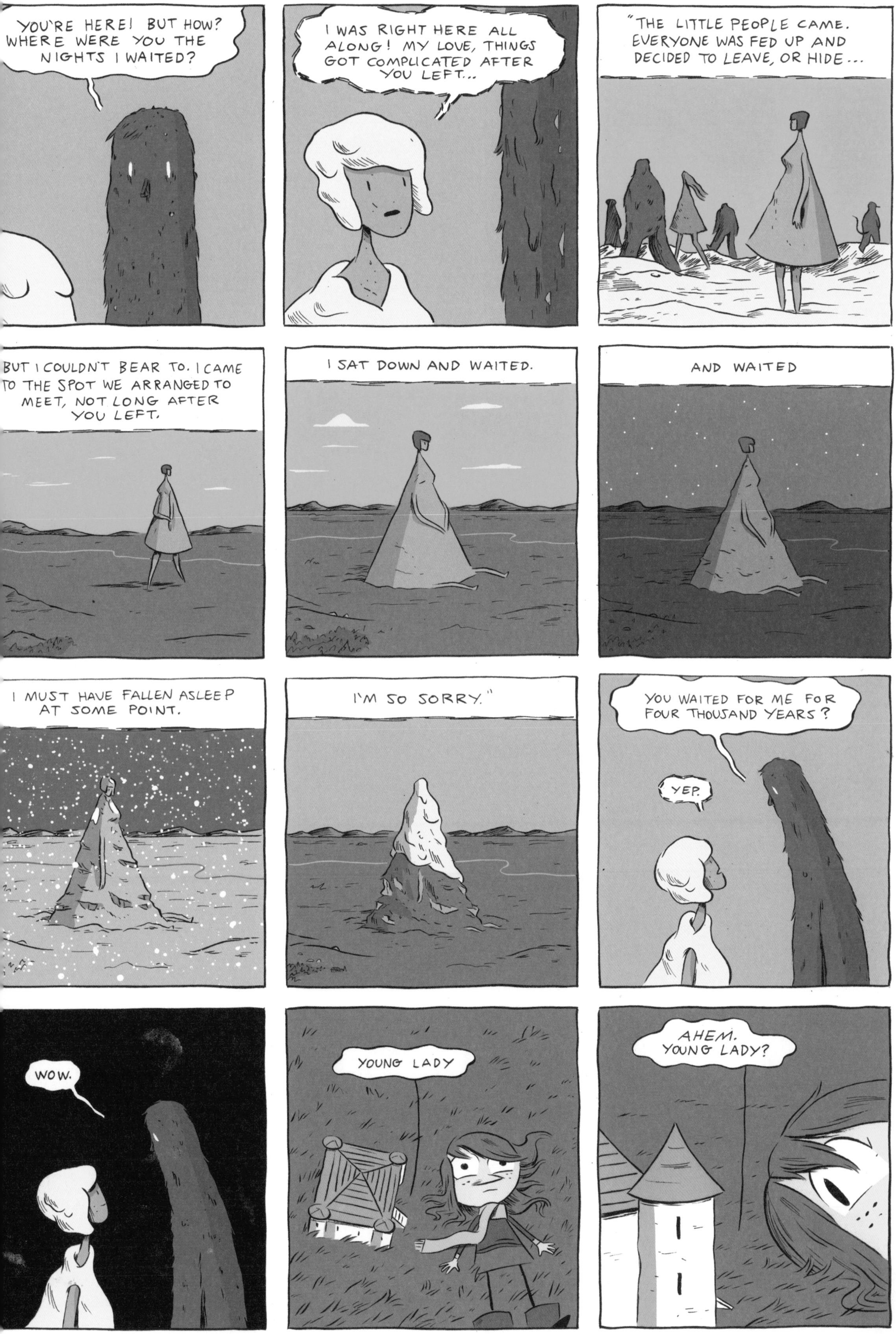
YOU'RE HERE! BUT HOW? WHERE WERE YOU THE NIGHTS I WAITED?
I WAS RIGHT HERE ALL ALONG! MY LOVE, THINGS GOT COMPLICATED AFTER YOU LEFT...
"THE LITTLE PEOPLE CAME. EVERYONE WAS FED UP AND DECIDED TO LEAVE, OR HIDE...
BUT I COULDN'T BEAR TO. I CAME TO THE SPOT WE ARRANGED TO MEET, NOT LONG AFTER YOU LEFT.
I SAT DOWN AND WAITED.
AND WAITED
I MUST HAVE FALLEN ASLEEP AT SOME POINT.
I'M SO SORRY."
YOU WAITED FOR ME FOR FOUR THOUSAND YEARS?
YEP.
WOW.
YOUNG LADY
AHEM. YOUNG LADY?

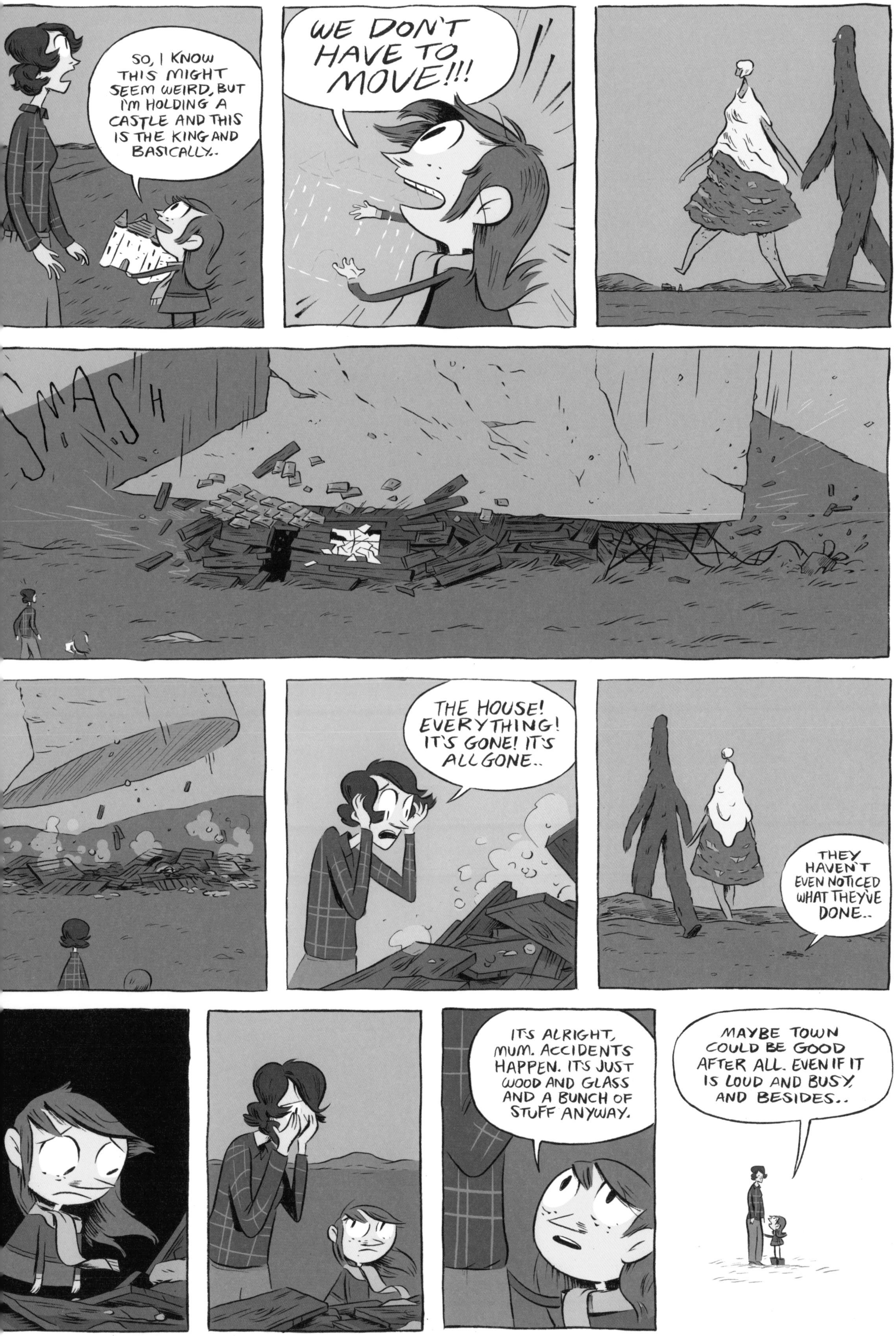
SO, I KNOW THIS MIGHT SEEM WEIRD, BUT I'M HOLDING A CASTLE AND THIS IS THE KING AND BASICALLY..
WE DON'T HAVE TO MOVE!!!
SMASH
THE HOUSE! EVERYTHING! IT'S GONE! IT'S ALL GONE..
THEY HAVEN'T EVEN NOTICED WHAT THEY'VE DONE..
IT'S ALRIGHT, MUM. ACCIDENTS HAPPEN. IT'S JUST WOOD AND GLASS AND A BUNCH OF STUFF ANYWAY.
MAYBE TOWN COULD BE GOOD AFTER ALL. EVEN IF IT IS LOUD AND BUSY, AND BESIDES..

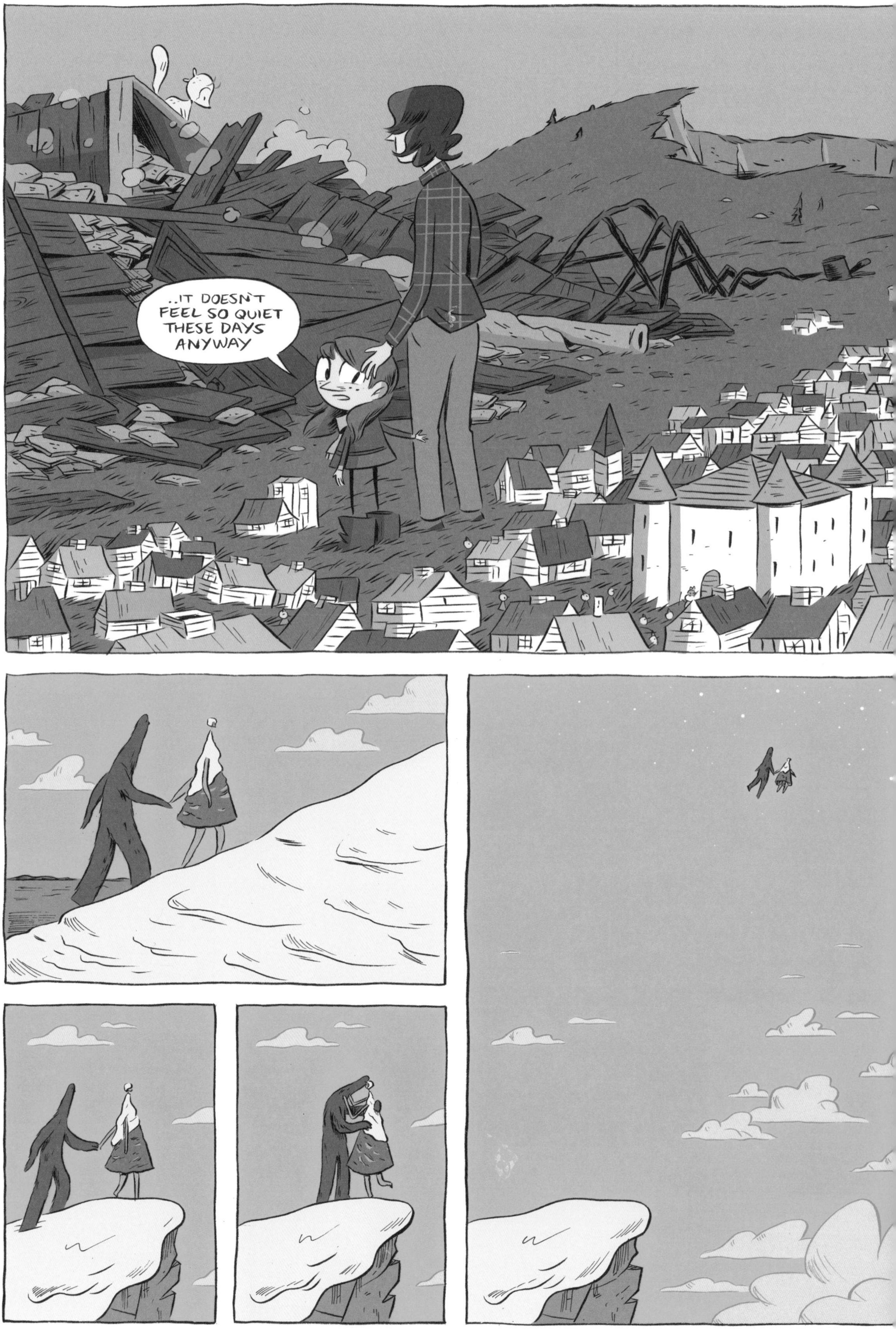
..IT DOESN'T FEEL SO QUIET THESE DAYS ANYWAY

This is a second edition printed 2012.
Hilda and the Midnight Giant is © 2011 Nobrow Ltd.

All artwork and characters within are © 2011 Luke Pearson and Nobrow Ltd.

Published by: Nobrow Ltd. 62 Great Eastern Street, London, EC2A 3QR
Design by Sam Arthur and Alex Spiro

Printed in Belgium on FSC assured paper

ISBN: 978-1-907704-25-3

Order from www.nobrow.net

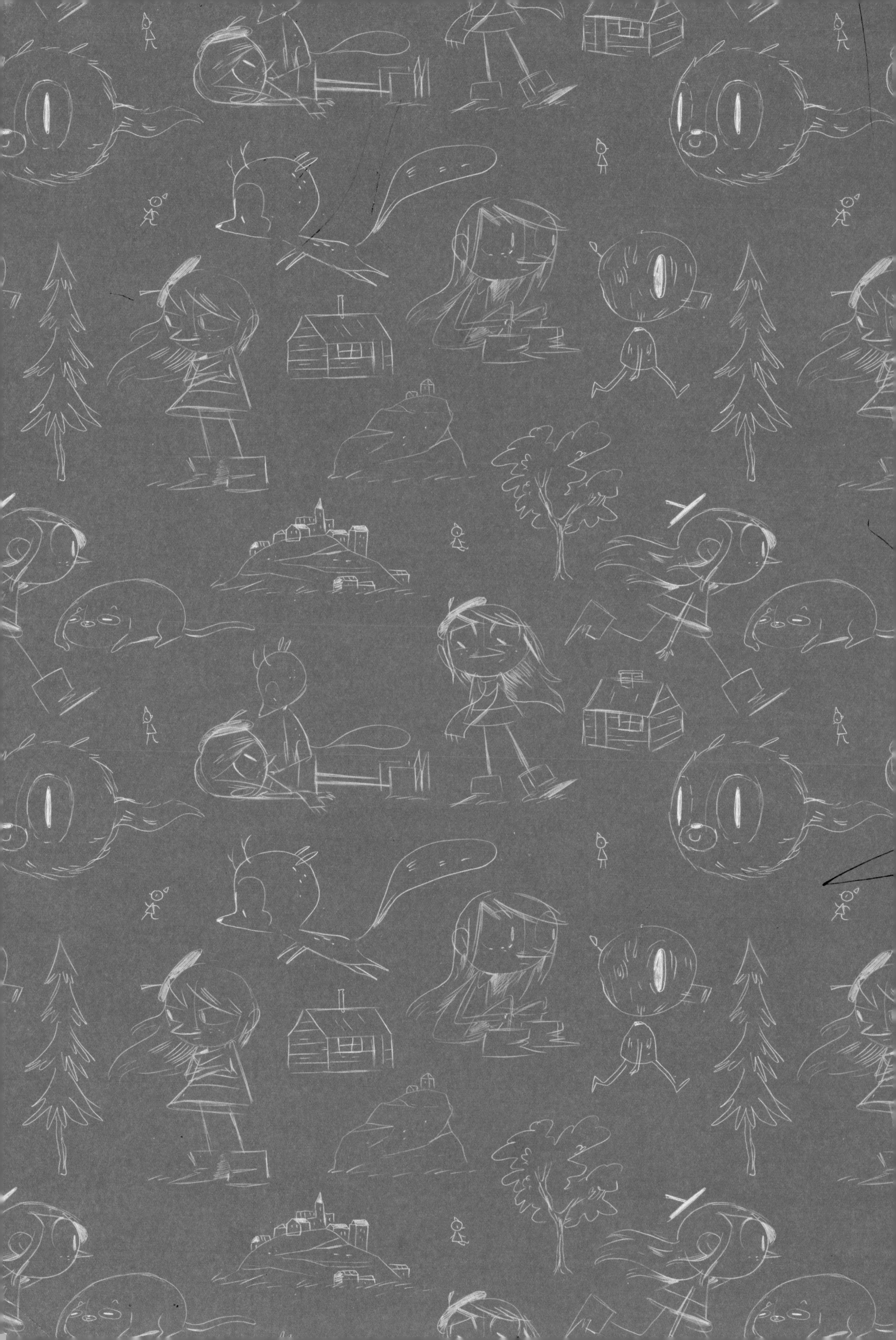